Tales from Shakespeare

Romeo and Juliet
&
Much Ado About Nothing

悅讀莎士比亞故事 (5)

羅。密。歐。與。茱。麗。葉。

無。事。生。非。

Charles and Mary Lamb

CONTENTS

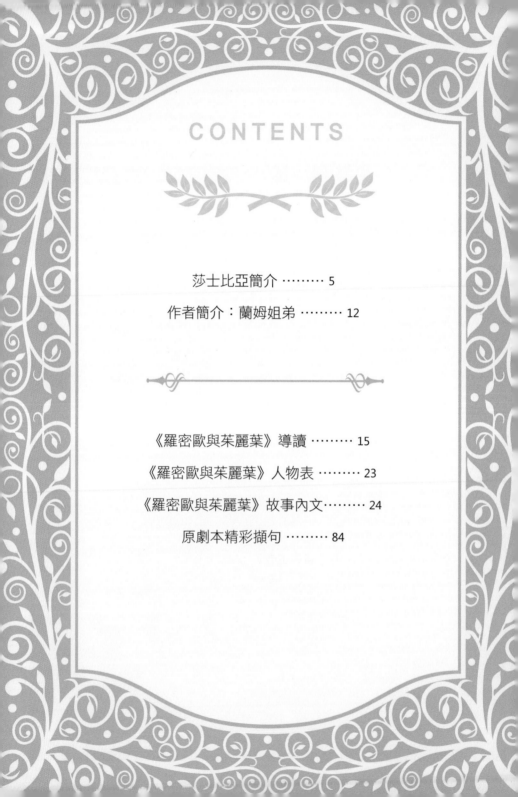

CONTENTS

附本

《羅密歐與茱麗葉》Practice

《無事生非》Practice

《羅密歐與茱麗葉》中譯

《無事生非》中譯

威廉・莎士比亞（William Shakespeare, 1564-1616）

Shakespeare Centre, Henley St, Stratford-upon-Avon, Warwickshire

莎士比亞簡介

陳敬旻

威廉・莎士比亞（William Shakespeare）出生於英國的史特拉福（Stratford-upon-Avon）。莎士比亞的父親曾任地方議員，母親是地主的女兒。莎士比亞對婦女在廚房或起居室裡勞動的描繪不少，這大概是經由觀察母親所得。他本人也懂得園藝，故作品中的植草種樹表現鮮活。

1571 年，莎士比亞進入公立學校就讀，校內教學多採拉丁文，因此在其作品中到處可見到羅馬詩人奧維德（Ovid）的影子。當時代古典文學的英譯日漸普遍，有學者認為莎士比亞只懂得英語，但這種說法有可議之處。舉例來說，在高登的譯本裡，森林女神只用 Diana 這個名字，而莎士比亞卻在《仲夏夜之夢》一劇中用奧維德原作中的 Titania 一名來稱呼仙后。和莎士比亞有私交的文學家班・強生（Ben Jonson）則曾說，莎翁「懂得一點拉丁文，和一點點希臘文」。

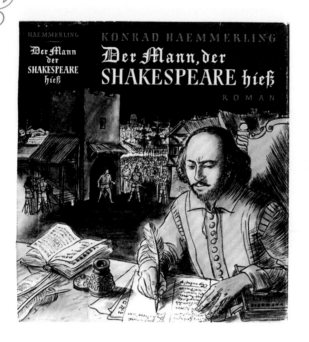

莎士比亞的劇本亦常引用聖經典故，顯示他對新舊約也頗為熟悉。
在伊麗莎白女王時期，通俗英語中已有很多聖經詞語。此外，莎士
比亞應該很知悉當時代年輕人所流行的遊戲娛樂，當時也應該有巡
迴劇團不時前來史特拉福演出。 1575 年，伊麗莎白女王來到郡上
時，當地人以化裝遊行、假面戲劇、煙火來款待女王，《仲夏夜之
夢》裡就有這種盛會的描繪。

1582 年，莎士比亞與安·海瑟威（Anne Hathaway）結婚，但這場
婚姻顯得草率，連莎士比亞的雙親都因不知情而沒有出席婚禮。
1586 年，他們在倫敦定居下來。 1586 年的倫敦已是英國首都，年
輕人莫不想在此大展抱負。史特拉福與倫敦之間的交通頻仍，但對
身無長物的人而言，步行仍是最平常的旅行方式。伊麗莎白時期的
文學家喜好步行， 1618 年，班·強生就曾在倫敦與愛丁堡之間徒步
來回。

莎士比亞初抵倫敦的史料不充足，引發諸多揣測。其中一説為莎士比亞曾在律師處當職員，因為他在劇本與詩歌中經常提及法律術語。但這種説法站不住腳，因為莎士比亞多有訛用，例如他在《威尼斯商人》和《一報還一報》中提到的法律原理及程序，就有諸多錯誤。

事實上，伊麗莎白時期的作家都喜歡引用法律詞彙，這是因為當時的文人和律師時有往來，而且中產階級也常介入訴訟案件，許多法律術語自然為常人所知。莎士比亞樂於援用法律術語，這顯示了他對當代生活和風尚的興趣。莎士比亞自抵達倫敦到告老還鄉，心思始終放在戲劇和詩歌上，不太可能接受法律這門專業領域的訓練。

莎士比亞在倫敦的第一份工作是劇場工作。當時常態營業的劇場有兩個：「劇場」（the Theatre）和「帷幕」（the Curtain）。「劇場」的所有人為詹姆士・波比奇（James Burbage），莎士比亞就在此落腳。「劇場」財務狀況不佳，1596 年波比奇過世，把「劇場」交給兩個兒子，其中一個兒子便是著名的悲劇演員理查・波比奇（Richard Burbage）。後來「劇場」因租約問題無法解決，決定將原有的建築物拆除，在泰晤士河的對面重建，改名為「環球」（the Globe）。不久，「環球」就展開了戲劇史上空前繁榮的時代。

伊麗莎白時期的戲劇表演只有男演員，所有的女性角色都由男性擔任。演員反串時會戴上面具，效果十足，然而這並不損故事的意境。莎士比亞本身也是一位出色的演員，曾在《皆大歡喜》和《哈姆雷特》中分別扮演忠僕亞當和國王鬼魂這兩個角色。

莎士比亞很留意演員的說白道詞，這點可從哈姆雷特告誡伶人的對話中窺知一二。莎士比亞熟稔劇場的技術與運作，加上他也是劇場股東，故對劇場的營運和組織都甚有研究。不過，他的志業不在演出或劇場管理，而是劇本和詩歌創作。

莎士比亞的戲劇創作始於 1591 年，他當時真正師法的對象是擅長喜劇的約翰·李利（John Lyly），以及曾寫下轟動一時的悲劇《帖木兒大帝》（*Tamburlaine the Great*）的克里斯多夫·馬婁（Christopher Marlowe）。莎翁戲劇的特色是兼容並蓄，吸收各家長處，而且他也勤奮多產。一直到 1611 年封筆之前，他每年平均寫出兩部劇作和三卷詩作。莎士比亞慣於在既有的文學作品中尋找材料，又重視大眾喜好，常能讓平淡無奇的作品廣受喜愛。

在當時，劇本都是賣斷給劇場，不能再賣給出版商，因此莎劇的出版先後，並不能反映其創作的時間先後。莎翁作品的先後順序都由後人所推斷，推測的主要依據是作品題材和韻格。他早期的戲劇作品，無論悲劇或喜劇，性質都很單純。隨著創作的手法逐漸成熟，內容愈來愈複雜深刻，悲喜劇熔冶一爐。

自 1591 年席德尼爵士（Sir Philip Sidney）的十四行詩集發表後，十四行詩（sonnets，另譯為商籟）在英國即普遍受到文人的喜愛與仿傚。其中許多作品承續佩脫拉克（Petrarch）的風格，多描寫愛情的酸甜苦樂。莎士比亞的創作一向很能反應當時代的文學風尚，在詩歌體裁鼎盛之時，他也將才華展現在十四行詩上，並將部分作品寫入劇本之中。

莎士比亞的十四行詩主要有兩個主題：婚姻責任和詩歌的不朽。這兩者皆是文藝復興時期詩歌中常見的主題。不少人以為莎士比亞的十四行詩表達了他個人的自省與懺悔，但事實上這些內容有更多是源於他的戲劇天分。

1595 年至 1598 年，莎士比亞陸續寫了《羅密歐與茱麗葉》、《仲夏夜之夢》、《馴悍記》、《威尼斯商人》和若干歷史劇，他的詩歌戲劇也在這段時期受到肯定。當時代的梅爾斯（Francis Meres）就將莎士比亞視為最偉大的文學家，他說：「要是繆思會說英語，一定也會喜歡引用莎士比亞的精彩語藻。」「無論是悲劇或喜劇，莎士比亞的表現都是首屈一指。」

闊別故鄉十一年後，莎士比亞於 1596 年返回故居，並在隔年買下名為「新居」（New Place）的房子。那是鎮上第二大的房子，他大幅改建整修，爾後家道日益興盛。莎士比亞有足夠的財力置產並不足以為奇，但他大筆的固定收入主要來自表演，而非劇本創作。當時不乏有成功的演員靠演戲發財，甚至有人將這種現象寫成劇本。

除了表演之外，劇場行政及管理的工作，還有宮廷演出的賞賜，都是他的財源。許多文獻均顯示，莎士比亞是個非常關心財富、地產和社會地位的人，讓許多人感到與他的詩人形象有些扞格不入。

伊麗莎白女王過世後，詹姆士一世（James I）於 1603 年登基，他把莎士比亞所屬的劇團納入保護。莎士比亞此時寫了《第十二夜》和佳評如潮的《哈姆雷特》，成就傲視全英格蘭。但他仍謙恭有禮、溫文爾雅，一如十多前年初抵倫敦的樣子，因此也愈發受到大眾的喜愛。

從這一年起，莎士比亞開始撰寫悲劇《奧賽羅》。他寫悲劇並非是因為精神壓力或生活變故，而是身為一名劇作家，最終目的就是要寫出優秀的悲劇作品。當時他嘗試以詩入劇，在《哈姆雷特》和《一報還一報》中尤其爐火純青。隨後《李爾王》和《馬克白》問世，一直到四年後的《安東尼與克麗奧佩脫拉》，寫作風格登峰造極。

1609 年，倫敦瘟疫猖獗，隔年不見好轉，46 歲的莎士比亞決定告別倫敦，返回史特拉福退隱。 1616 年，莎士比亞和老友德雷頓、班·強生聚會時，可能由於喝得過於盡興，回家後發高燒，一病不起。他將遺囑修改完畢，同年 4 月 23 日，恰巧在他 52 歲的生日當天去世。

七年後，昔日的劇團好友收錄他的劇本做為全集出版，其中有喜劇、歷史劇、悲劇等共 36 個劇本。此書不僅不負莎翁本人所託，也為後人留下珍貴而豐富的文化資源，其中不僅包括美妙動人的詞句，還有各種人物的性格塑造，如高貴、低微、嚴肅或歡樂等性格的著墨。

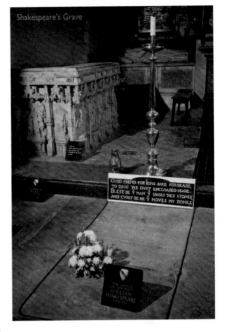

除了作品，莎士比亞本人也在生前受到讚揚。班·強生曾說他是個「正人君子，天性開放自由，想像力出奇，擁有大無畏的思想，言詞溫和，蘊含機智。」也有學者以勇敢、敏感、平衡、幽默和身心健康這五種特質來形容莎士比亞，並說他「將無私的愛奉為至上，認為罪惡的根源是恐懼，而非金錢。」

值得一提的是，有人認為這些劇本刻畫入微，具有知性，不可能是未受過大學教育的莎士比亞所寫，因而引發爭議。有人就此推測真正的作者，其中較為人知的有法蘭西斯·培根（Francis Bacon）和牛津的德維爾公爵（Edward de Vere of Oxford），後者形成了頗具影響力的牛津學派。儘管傳說繪聲繪影，各種假說和研究不斷，但大概已經沒有人會懷疑確有莎士比亞這個人的存在了。

作者簡介：蘭姆姐弟

陳敬旻

姐姐瑪麗（Mary Lamb）生於 1764 年，弟弟查爾斯（Charles Lamb）於 1775 年也在倫敦呱呱落地。因為家境不夠寬裕，瑪麗沒有接受過完整的教育。她從小就做針線活，幫忙持家，照顧母親。查爾斯在學生時代結識了詩人柯立芝（Samuel Taylor Coleridge），兩人成為終生的朋友。查爾斯後來因家中經濟困難而輟學， 1792 年轉而就職於東印度公司（East India House），這是他謀生的終身職業。

查爾斯在二十歲時一度精神崩潰，瑪麗則因為長年工作過量，在 1796 年突然精神病發，持刀攻擊父母，母親不幸傷重身亡。這件人倫悲劇發生後，瑪麗被判為精神異常，送往精神病院。查爾斯為此放棄自己原本期待的婚姻，以便全心照顧姐姐，使她免於在精神病院終老。

十九世紀的英國教育重視莎翁作品，一般的中產階級家庭也希望孩子早點接觸莎劇。1806 年，文學家兼編輯高德溫（William Godwin）邀請查爾斯協助「少年圖書館」的出版計畫，請他將莎翁的劇本改寫為適合兒童閱讀的故事。

查爾斯接受這項工作後就與瑪麗合作，他負責六齣悲劇，瑪麗負責十四齣喜劇並撰寫前言。瑪麗在後來曾描述說，他們兩人「就坐在同一張桌子上改寫，看起來就好像《仲夏夜之夢》裡的荷米雅與海蓮娜一樣。」就這樣，姐弟兩人合力完成了這一系列的莎士比亞故事。《莎士比亞故事集》在 1807 年出版後便大受好評，建立了查爾斯的文學聲譽。

查爾斯的寫作風格獨特，筆法樸實，主題豐富。他將自己的一生，包括童年時代、基督教會學校的生活、東印度公司的光陰、與瑪麗相伴的點點滴滴，以及自己的白日夢、鍾愛的書籍和友人等等，都融入在文章裡，作品充滿細膩情感和豐富的想像力。他的軟弱、怪異、魅力、幽默、口吃，在在都使讀者感到親切熟悉，而獨特的筆法與敘事方式，也使他成為英國出色的散文大師。

1823 年，查爾斯和瑪麗領養了一個孤兒愛瑪。兩年後，查爾斯自東印度公司退休，獲得豐厚的退休金。查爾斯的健康情形和瑪麗的精神狀況卻每況愈下。 1833 年，愛瑪嫁給出版商後，又只剩下姐弟兩人。 1834 年 7 月，由於幼年時代的好友柯立芝去世，查爾斯的精神一蹶不振，沉湎酒精。此年秋天，查爾斯在散步時不慎跌倒，傷及顏面，後來傷口竟惡化至不可收拾的地步，而於年底過世。

查爾斯善與人交，他和同時期的許多文人都保持良好情誼，又因他一生對姐姐的照顧不餘遺力，所以也廣受敬佩。查爾斯和瑪麗兩人都終生未婚，查爾斯曾在一篇伊利亞小品中，將他們的狀況形容為「雙重單身」（double singleness）。查爾斯去世後，瑪麗的心理狀態雖然漸趨惡化，但仍繼續活了十三年之久。

Romeo
and Juliet

羅密歐與茱麗葉

導讀

陳敬旻

劇情架構

《羅密歐與茱麗葉》是莎士比亞很受歡迎的劇作。根據推測,本劇完成於 1596 年,故事源自十六世紀的義大利小說,敘述秘密戀情受到家庭、命運或死亡等限制,或感受到時間的緊迫與壓力而造成不幸結局。

莎士比亞創作此劇的主要來源有兩個:
1. Arthur Brooks 的《羅密額斯與茱麗葉的悲劇史》
   (*Tragicall Historye of Romeus and Juliet*)
2. William Painter 的《羅密歐與茱麗葉塔》
   (*Rhomeo and Julietta*)

前者尤其提供了故事完整的架構,因此莎翁的《羅》劇幾乎可說是依據該作品改寫而成。本劇描述維洛那城的兩個望族孟鐵古與柯譜雷,兩家為世仇,但兩家子女羅密歐與茱麗葉卻在一場舞會中墜入情網,並透過修士勞倫斯的證婚,秘密結為夫婦。

完婚當天,兩家人馬在街上鬥毆,柯家的提伯特殺死了羅密歐的好友馬庫修,羅密歐一時激憤,也殺了提伯特。維洛那親王於是下令驅逐羅密歐。

之後，茱麗葉的父親提出一門親事，要她嫁給裴力司伯爵。無助的茱麗葉向勞倫斯修士求助，並接受他的提議喝下一種藥水，以便詐死。修士打算把這個消息告訴羅密歐，叫他到墓穴裡把茱麗葉帶走，但羅密歐始終沒有接到修士的信，只得知茱麗葉死去的消息。他萬分悲痛，當晚趕回維洛那城，服毒殉情。茱麗葉醒來後，看到身旁的羅密歐已經殉情而死，於是就用短劍結束自己的生命。

故事中的愛情簡單而真誠、衝動而自然，故事中的仇恨則是直接而暴力，此種情感和其他的莎劇有顯著不同。本劇的主角都是青少年（羅密歐十八歲，茱麗葉十三歲），情感的方式直接外放，充滿年少情懷。羅密歐在一開場就是個深陷情網、為愛癡狂的年輕人，在遇見茱麗葉之後，又立刻為之瘋狂。他翻越柯家圍牆，遂產生了著名的「樓台景」（the balcony scene）。當他後來知道自己被放逐了以後，整個人癱在地上嚎啕大哭，而茱麗葉對自己情感的表白也同樣直率。

隨著故事的發展，兩人陷入孤立狀況。除了勞倫斯修士，親友都不知道他們的戀情，兩人只能獨自面對苦戀、家庭和逼婚的壓力，還有墓地的恐怖景象。

「命」與「運」

本劇雖然是莎翁早期的悲劇，但從中已經隱約可見莎氏悲劇的雛型：「運」（fortune）與「命」（nature）交織，構成悲劇的因果。例如，勞倫斯修士的信未曾送達羅密歐的手裡，而羅密歐則在衝動的性格下飲鴆自盡。劇中有多處顯示，羅密歐雖有好想法，卻總是缺乏機運，加以行事過於魯莽，終究步入無可挽救的田地。因此，也有不少評論家認為茱麗葉顯得較為成熟懂事，她對自己的感情誠實，但不直接違抗父命，對裴力司持適當的禮儀，並有勇氣接受勞倫斯修士的建議，以維護自己的婚姻。

婚姻這一點也反映出清教徒重視神聖婚姻的傳統。在英國詩人喬叟（Geoffrey Chaucer, 1345-1400）、史賓賽（Edmund Spenser, 1552?-1599）或義大利詩人佩托拉克（Petrarch, 1304-1374）的故事裡，都可見男性追求理想女子的最終目的就是結婚。在伊莉莎白時期，男生合法的結婚年齡為十四歲，女生則為十二歲。在望族之中，女孩出嫁的年齡會更小，這是因為父母為確保其地位財產，會提早為女兒安排婚事，而這也是茱麗葉所面臨的狀況。

本故事最常見的評論是關於命運與意志的衝突，莎翁在此劇裡把兩者放在同等的地位上。對於羅密歐和茱麗葉的悲劇命運，批評家有各種看法。羅勒（John Lawlor）從中古世紀悲劇的標準來看，指出命運並不企圖控制人類，但人若願意從命運的教訓中學習，則可化解悲劇的結果，例如兩大家族最後化解了彼此的仇恨。

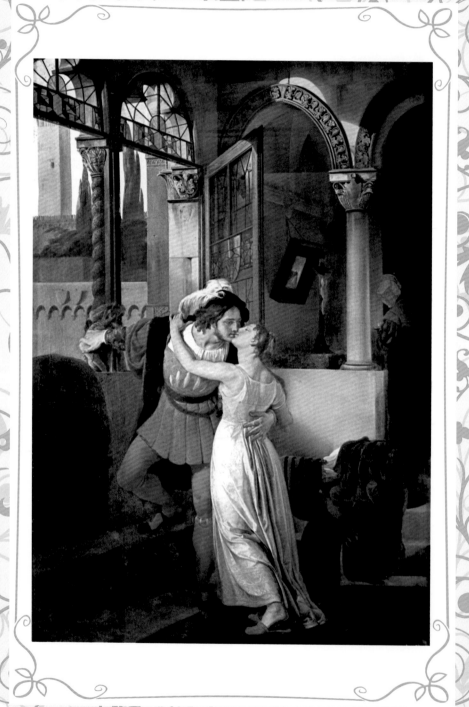

愛情的欲望

劇中也有多處呈現觀念的衝突和愛情的矛盾。例如：茱麗葉既承認自己的感情，卻又認為表白過於露骨；勞倫斯修士既希望男女主角的結合可以消除兩家的世仇，卻又擔心激情會害了兩人。莎士比亞將這股對愛情的欲望用悲劇作為結束，恰巧顯示了人們對伊莉莎白時期的浪漫主義思想，有著焦慮悲觀的一面。

人們對欲望的態度會反映出其社會文化，茱麗葉在樓台一景的自我表白，不同於傳統中否定欲望的態度。在當時，女性對愛情的欲望象徵著死亡，但男女主角基於欲望的相許，也為浪漫的個人主義樹立了新觀點。劇中男女主角年紀輕輕就受到愛欲驅使，私下結婚。這股個人的欲望又和父權產生衝突，因為當時的父親有權為女兒安排婚事。

克里伯（T. J. Cribb）以新柏拉圖的觀念來看本劇的秩序，例如「死亡」代表愛情勝過仇恨，愛與恨這兩種相抗的力量由提伯特這個角色來表現：他反對這對戀人，卻讓他們成為愛情英雄。浪漫時期的作家特別讚揚此劇，如華茲華斯（William Wordsworth）、柯立芝（Samuel Taylor Coleridge）、雪萊（Percy Bysshe Shelley）、濟慈（John Keats）、蘭姆（Charles Lamb）或韓茲黎（William Hazlitt）。但二十世紀的批評家如卜瑞黎（A. C. Bradley）則傾向於認為，比起莎翁晚期的作品如《李爾王》、《馬克白》等，此劇顯得缺乏力量與深度，不夠成熟。

語言的表現

除了情節和人物之外，本劇的語言也特別受到重視。莎翁在這個時期偏好人物描寫和詩藝。當時盛行十四行詩，他也用這種修辭語言來表現表現戀人的心境。這種寫作方式包括誇飾（hyperbole）、機智言詞（witty conceit）、似是而非的謔辭（oxymoron）和反覆（repetition）等等，而其寫作內容則刻意表現出模糊、暗示和預言。也因此如此，所以劇中有些對話不像是在刻畫角色，反倒像是一段詩作。

人物表

Romeo	羅密歐	孟家的愛子
Juliet	茱麗葉	柯家的愛女，柯家與孟家是世仇
Benvolio	班夫禮	羅密歐的友人
Mercutio	馬庫修	羅密歐的友人
Tybalt	提伯特	柯家人，茱麗葉的堂兄
Friar Lawrence	勞倫斯修士	主持歐密歐和茱麗葉的婚禮
Paris	裴力司伯爵	父親挑選的女婿，要與茱麗葉結婚

Romeo and Juliet

The two chief families in Verona were the rich Capulets and the Montagues. There had been an old quarrel between these families, which was grown to such a height, and so deadly was the enmity[1] between them, that it extended to the remotest kindred, to the followers and retainers[2] of both sides, insomuch that a servant of the house of Montague could not meet a servant of the house of Capulet, nor a Capulet encounter with a Montague by chance, but fierce words and sometimes bloodshed ensued[3]; and frequent were the brawls[4] from such accidental meetings, which disturbed the happy quiet of Verona's streets.

Old Lord Capulet made a great supper, to which many fair ladies and many noble guests were invited. All the admired beauties of Verona were present, and all comers were made welcome if they were not of the house of Montague.

1 enmity ['enmɪti] (n.) 仇恨
2 retainer [rɪ'teɪnər] (n.) 〔舊時用法〕僕人
3 ensue [ɪn'suː] (v.) 隨著發生
4 brawl [brɑːl] (n.) 大聲的爭吵

🎧 At this feast of Capulets, Rosaline, beloved of Romeo, son to the old Lord Montague, was present; and though it was dangerous for a Montague to be seen in this assembly, yet Benvolio, a friend of Romeo, persuaded the young lord to go to this assembly in the disguise of a mask, that he might see his Rosaline, and seeing her, compare her with some choice beauties of Verona, who (he said) would make him think his swan a crow.

Romeo had small faith in Benvolio's words; nevertheless, for the love of Rosaline, he was persuaded to go. For Romeo was a sincere and passionate lover, and one that lost his sleep for love, and fled society to be alone, thinking on Rosaline, who disdained[5] him, and never requited his love, with the least show of courtesy or affection; and Benvolio wished to cure his friend of this love by showing him diversity of ladies and company.

To this feast of Capulets then young Romeo with Benvolio and their friend Mercutio went masked. Old Capulet bid them welcome, and told them that ladies who had their toes unplagued[6] with corns[7] would dance with them. And the old man was light hearted and merry, and said that he had worn a mask when he was young, and could have told a whispering tale in a fair lady's ear.

5 disdain [dɪsˈdeɪn] (v.) 藐視
6 unplagued [ʌnˈpleɪgd] (a.) 未受苦的
7 corn [kɔːrn] (n.) 雞眼

ROMEO.   What lady is that, which doth
          enrich the hand of yonder knight?
Servant. I know not, sir.

🎧 3 And they fell to dancing, and Romeo was suddenly struck with the exceeding beauty of a lady who danced there, who seemed to him to teach the torches to burn bright, and her beauty to show by night like a rich jewel worn by a blackamoor[8]; beauty too rich for use, too dear for earth! like a snowy dove trooping with crows (he said), so richly did her beauty and perfections shine above the ladies her companions.

While he uttered these praises, he was overheard by Tybalt, a nephew of Lord Capulet, who knew him by his voice to be Romeo. And this Tybalt, being of a fiery[9] and passionate temper, could not endure that a Montague should come under cover of a mask, to fleer[10] and scorn (as he said) at their solemnities. And he stormed and raged exceedingly, and would have struck young Romeo dead.

But his uncle, the old Lord Capulet, would not suffer him to do any injury at that time, both out of respect to his guests, and because Romeo had borne himself like a gentleman, and all tongues in Verona bragged of him to be a virtuous and well-governed youth.

8 blackamoor [ˈblækəmuə] (n.) 〔輕蔑用法〕黑人
9 fiery [ˈfaɪrɪ] (a.) 易怒的；暴躁的
10 fleer [flɪr] (v.) 嘲笑

🎧 Tybalt, forced to be patient against his will, restrained himself, but swore that this vile Montague should at another time dearly pay for his intrusion.

The dancing being done, Romeo watched the place where the lady stood; and under favor of his masking habit, which might seem to excuse in part the liberty, he presumed[11] in the gentlest manner to take her by the hand, calling it a shrine, which if he profaned[12] by touching it, he was a blushing pilgrim, and would kiss it for atonement[13].

"Good pilgrim," answered the lady, "your devotion shows by far too mannerly and too courtly: saints have hands, which pilgrims may touch, but kiss not."

"Have not saints lips, and pilgrims, too?" said Romeo.

"Ay," said the lady, "lips which they must use in prayer."

"Oh, then, my dear saint," said Romeo, "hear my prayer, and grant it, lest I despair."

---

11 presume [prɪˈzuːm] (v.) 擅敢；冒昧
12 profane [prəˈfeɪn] (v.) 褻瀆
13 atonement [əˈtoʊnmənt] (n.) 彌補；贖罪

🎧5 　In such like allusions[14] and loving conceits[15] they were engaged, when the lady was called away to her mother. And Romeo inquiring who her mother was, discovered that the lady whose peerless beauty he was so much struck with, was young Juliet, daughter and heir to the Lord Capulet, the great enemy of the Montagues; and that he had unknowingly engaged his heart to his foe.

　This troubled him, but it could not dissuade[16] him from loving. As little rest had Juliet, when she found that the gentleman that she had been talking with was Romeo and a Montague, for she had been suddenly smit[17] with the same hasty and inconsiderate passion for Romeo, which he had conceived for her; and a prodigious[18] birth of love it seemed to her, that she must love her enemy, and that her affections should settle there, where family considerations should induce her chiefly to hate.

14 allusion [əˈluːʒən] (n.) 暗示；間接提及
15 conceit [kənˈsiːt] (n.) 詼諧機智的思想或語句
16 dissuade [dɪˈsweɪd] (v.) 勸阻
17 smit [smɪt] (v.) 痛擊
18 prodigious [prəˈdɪdʒəs] (a.) 奇異的

It being midnight, Romeo with his companions departed; but they soon missed him, for, unable to stay away from the house where he had left his heart, he leaped the wall of an orchard which was at the back of Juliet's house. Here he had not been long, ruminating[19] on his new love, when Juliet appeared above at a window, through which her exceeding beauty seemed to break like the light of the sun in the east; and the moon, which shone in the orchard with a faint light, appeared to Romeo as if sick and pale with grief at the superior luster[20] of this new sun.

And she, leaning her cheek upon her hand, he passionately wished himself a glove upon that hand, that he might touch her cheek. She all this while thinking herself alone, fetched a deep sigh, and exclaimed, "Ah me!"

Romeo, enraptured[21] to bear her speak, said softly, and unheard by her, "Oh, speak again, bright angel, for such you appear, being over my head, like a winged messenger from heaven whom mortals fall back to gaze upon."

---

19 ruminate ['ruːmɪneɪt] (v.) 反覆思索
20 luster ['lʌstər] (n.) 光澤；光輝
21 enraptured [ɪn'ræptʃərd] (a.) 狂喜的

ROMEO.   But, soft! what light through yonder window breaks?
          It is the east, and Juliet is the sun.

🎧7 She, unconscious of being overheard, and full of the new passion which that night's adventure had given birth to, called upon her lover by name (whom she supposed absent): "Oh, Romeo, Romeo!" said she, "wherefore²² art thou Romeo? Deny thy father, and refuse thy name, for my sake; or if thou wilt not, be but my sworn love, and I no longer will be a Capulet."

22 wherefore [ˈwerfɔːr] (adv.) 〔舊時用法〕為何

8 Romeo, having this encouragement, would fain have spoken, but he was desirous of hearing more; and the lady continued her passionate discourse with herself (as she thought), still chiding Romeo for being Romeo and a Montague, and wishing him some other name, or that he would put away that hated name, and for that name which was no part of himself, he should take all herself.

At this loving word Romeo could no longer refrain[23], but taking up the dialogue as if her words had been addressed to him personally, and not merely in fancy, he bade her call him Love, or by whatever other name she pleased, for he was no longer Romeo, if that name was displeasing to her.

23 refrain [rɪˈfreɪn] (v.) 克制

🎧⁹ Juliet, alarmed to hear a man's voice in the garden, did not at first know who it was, that by favor of the night and darkness had thus stumbled upon the discovery of her secret; but when he spoke again, though her ears had not yet drunk a hundred words of that tongue's uttering, yet so nice is a lover's hearing, that she immediately knew him to be young Romeo, and she expostulated[24] with him on the danger to which he had exposed himself by climbing the orchard walls, for if any of her kinsmen should find him there, it would be death to him being a Montague.

"Alack!" said Romeo, "there is more peril in your eye, than in twenty of their swords. Do you but look kind upon me, lady, and I am proof against their enmity. Better my life should be ended by their hate, than that hated life should be prolonged, to live without your love."

"How came you into this place," said Juliet, "and by whose direction?"

"Love directed me," answered Romeo. "I am no pilot, yet wert thou as far apart from me, as that vast shore which is washed with the farthest sea, I should venture for such merchandise."

---

24 expostulate [ɪkˈspɑːstʃuleɪt] (v.) 告誡；勸誡

Act 2. Scene 3.

A crimson[25] blush came over Juliet's face, yet unseen by Romeo by reason of the night, when she reflected upon the discovery which she had made, yet not meaning to make it, of her love to Romeo. She would fain have recalled her words, but that was impossible; fain would she have stood upon form, and have kept her lover at a distance, as the custom of discreet[26] ladies is, to frown and be perverse[27], and give their suitors harsh denials at first; to stand off, and affect a coyness[28] or indifference, where they most love, that their lovers may not think them too lightly or too easily won; for the difficulty of attainment increases the value of the object.

---

25 crimson ['krɪmzən] (a.) 深紅色的
26 discreet [dɪ'skriːt] (a.) 謹慎的
27 perverse [pər'vɜːrs] (a.) 故意作惡的
28 coyness ['kɔɪnɪs] (n.) 害羞；嬌羞忸怩

🎧 But there was no room in her case for denials, or puttings off, or any of the customary arts of delay and protracted[29] courtship. Romeo had heard from her own tongue, when she did not dream that he was near her, a confession of her love. So with an honest frankness, which the novelty of her situation excused, she confirmed the truth of what he had before heard, and addressing him by the name of *Fair Montague* (love can sweeten a sour name), she begged him not to impute[30] her easy yielding to levity[31] or an unworthy mind, but that he must lay the fault of it (if it were a fault) upon the accident of the night which had so strangely discovered her thoughts.

And she added, that though her behavior to him might not be sufficiently prudent[32], measured by the custom of her sex, yet that she would prove more true than many whose prudence was dissembling[33], and their modesty artificial cunning.

29 protracted [prə'træktɪd] (a.) 拖延時間的
30 impute [ɪm'pjuːt] (v.) 歸於
31 levity ['levɪti] (n.) 輕率
32 prudent ['pruːdənt] (a.) 審慎小心的
33 dissemble [dɪ'sembəl] (v.) 掩飾

🎧 12 Romeo was beginning to call the heavens to witness, that nothing was farther from his thoughts than to impute a shadow of dishonor to such an honored lady, when she stopped him, begging him not to swear; for although she joyed in him, yet she had no joy of that night's contract: it was too rash, too unadvised, too sudden.

But he being urgent with her to exchange a vow of love with him that night, she said that she already had given him hers before he requested it; meaning, when he overheard her confession; but she would retract what she then bestowed[34], for the pleasure of giving it again, for her bounty[35] was as infinite as the sea, and her love as deep.

From this loving conference she was called away by her nurse, who slept with her, and thought it time for her to be in bed, for it was near to daybreak; but hastily returning, she said three or four words more to Romeo, the purport[36] of which was, that if his love was indeed honorable, and his purpose marriage, she would send a messenger to him tomorrow, to appoint a time for their marriage, when she would lay all her fortunes at his feet, and follow him as her lord through the world.

---

34 bestow [bɪˈstoʊ] (v.) 賜與
35 bounty [ˈbaʊnti] (n.) 慷慨
36 purport [pɜːrˈpɔːrt] (n.) 主旨

🎧13 　While they were settling this point, Juliet was repeatedly called for by her nurse, and went in and returned, and went and returned again, for she seemed as jealous of Romeo going from her, as a young girl of her bird, which she will let hop a little from her hand, and pluck it back with a silken thread; and Romeo was as loath[37] to part as she; for the sweetest music to lovers is the sound of each other's tongues at night.

　But at last they parted, wishing mutually sweet sleep and rest for that night.

　The day was breaking when they parted, and Romeo, who was too full of thoughts of his mistress and that blessed meeting to allow him to sleep, instead of going home, bent his course to a monastery[38] hard by, to find Friar[39] Lawrence.

　The good friar was already up at his devotions, but seeing young Romeo abroad so early, he conjectured[40] rightly that he had not been abed that night, but that some distemper[41] of youthful affection had kept him waking.

---

37 loath [louθ] (a.) 不願意做某事
38 monastery [ˈmɑːnəsteri] (n.) 修道院
39 friar [ˈfraɪər] (n.) 修道士
40 conjecture [kənˈdʒektʃər] (v.) 猜想；推測
41 distemper [dɪˈstempər] (n.) 思緒混亂

FRIAR LAURENCE.
Now, ere the sun advance his burning eye,
The day to cheer and night's dank dew to dry,
I must up-fill this osier cage of ours
With baleful weeds and precious-juiced flowers.

Act 2. Scene 3.

🎧14 He was right in imputing the cause of Romeo's
wakefulness to love, but he made a wrong guess at
the object, for he thought that his love for Rosaline
had kept him waking.

But when Romeo revealed his new passion for
Juliet, and requested the assistance of the friar to
marry them that day, the holy man lifted up his eyes
and hands in a sort of wonder at the sudden change
in Romeo's affections, for he had been privy[42] to all
Romeo's love for Rosaline, and his many complaints
of her disdain; and he said, that young men's love lay
not truly in their hearts, but in their eyes.

42 privy ['prɪvi] (a.) 知情的

15 But Romeo replying, that he himself had often chidden[43] him for doting on Rosaline, who could not love him again, whereas Juliet both loved and was beloved by him, the friar assented in some measure to his reasons; and thinking that a matrimonial[44] alliance between young Juliet and Romeo might happily be the means of making up the long breach between the Capulets and the Montagues; which no one more lamented[45] than this good friar, who was a friend to both the families and had often interposed[46] his mediation to make up the quarrel without effect; partly moved by policy, and partly by his fondness for young Romeo, to whom he could deny nothing, the old man consented to join their hands in marriage.

43 chide [tʃaɪd] (v.) 責罵
44 matrimonial [ˌmætrɪˈmoʊniəl] (a.) 婚姻的
45 lament [ləˈment] (v.) 悲傷;惋惜
46 interpose [ˌɪntərˈpoʊz] (v.) 調停

🎧16 Now was Romeo blessed indeed, and Juliet, who
knew his intent from a messenger which she had
despatched[47] according to promise, did not fail to be
early at the cell of Friar Lawrence, where their hands
were joined in holy marriage; the good friar praying
the heavens to smile upon that act, and in the union
of this young Montague and young Capulet to bury
the old strife and long dissensions[48] of their families.

47 despatch [dɪˈspætʃ] (v.) 派遣
48 dissension [dɪˈsenʃən] (n.) 紛爭

JULIET.   But my true love is grown to such excess
          I cannot sum up sum of half my wealth.

Act 2. Scene 6.

The ceremony being over, Juliet hastened home, where she stayed impatient for the coming of night, at which time Romeo promised to come and meet her in the orchard, where they had met the night before; and the time between seemed as tedious to her, as the night before some great festival seems to an impatient child, that has got new finery which it may not put on till the morning.

🎧 ⟨18⟩ That same day, about noon, Romeo's friends, Benvolio and Mercutio, walking through the streets of Verona, were met by a party of the Capulets with the impetuous[49] Tybalt at their head. This was the same angry Tybalt who would have fought with Romeo at old Lord Capulet's feast.

He, seeing Mercutio, accused him bluntly of associating with Romeo, a Montague. Mercutio, who had as much fire and youthful blood in him as Tybalt, replied to this accusation with some sharpness; and in spite of all Benvolio could say to moderate[50] their wrath, a quarrel was beginning, when Romeo himself passing that way, the fierce Tybalt turned from Mercutio to Romeo, and gave him the disgraceful appellation[51] of villain[52].

Romeo wished to avoid a quarrel with Tybalt above all men, because he was the kinsman of Juliet, and much beloved by her; besides, this young Montague had never thoroughly entered into the family quarrel, being by nature wise and gentle, and the name of a Capulet, which was his dear lady's name, was now rather a charm to allay[53] resentment[54], than a watchword to excite fury.

---

49 impetuous [ɪmˈpetʃuəs] (a.) 衝動魯莽的
50 moderate [ˈmɑːdəreɪt] (v.) 緩和；減輕
51 appellation [ˌæpəˈleɪʃən] (n.) 名稱；稱呼
52 villain [ˈvɪlən] (n.) 惡徒
53 allay [əˈleɪ] (v.) 減輕；緩和
54 resentment [rɪˈzentmənt] (n.) 憤恨

🎧19   So he tried to reason with Tybalt, whom he saluted mildly by the name of *Good Capulet*, as if he, though Montague, had some secret pleasure in uttering that name; but Tybalt, who hated all Montagues as he hated hell, would hear no reason, but drew his weapon; and Mercutio, who knew not of Romeo's secret motive for desiring peace with Tybalt, but looked upon his present forbearance as a sort of calm dishonorable submission[55], with many disdainful words provoked[56] Tybalt to the prosecution[57] of his first quarrel with him; and Tybalt and Mercutio fought, till Mercutio fell, receiving his death's wound while Romeo and Benvolio were vainly endeavoring to part the combatants[58].

  Mercutio being dead, Romeo kept his temper no longer, but returned the scornful appellation of villain which Tybalt had given him; and they fought till Tybalt was slain[59] by Romeo.

---

[55] submission [səbˈmɪʃən] (n.) 服從；忠順
[56] provoke [prəˈvouk] (v.) 迫使
[57] prosecution [ˌprɑːsɪˈkjuːʃən] (n.) 進行；繼續從事
[58] combatant [kəmˈbætənt] (n.) 戰鬥人員
[59] slay [sle] (v.) 殺死（動詞變化：slew; slain; slaying）

🎧 ⟨20⟩ This deadly broil falling out in the midst of Verona at noonday, the news of it quickly brought a crowd of citizens to the spot, and among them the old Lords Capulet and Montague, with their wives; and soon after arrived the prince himself, who being related to Mercutio, whom Tybalt had slain, and having had the peace of his government often disturbed by these brawls of Montagues and Capulets, came determined to put the law in strictest force against those who should be found to be offenders.

Benvolio, who had been eye witness to the fray[60], was commanded by the prince to relate the origin of it, which he did, keeping as near the truth as he could without injury to Romeo, softening and excusing the part which his friends took in it.

Lady Capulet, whose extreme grief for the loss of her kinsman Tybalt made her keep no bounds in her revenge, exhorted[61] the prince to do strict justice upon his murderer, and to pay no attention to Benvolio's representation, who, being Romeo's friend and a Montague, spoke partially. Thus she pleaded[62] against her new son-in-law, but she knew not yet that he was her son-in-law and Juliet's husband.

---

60 fray [freɪ] (n.) 打鬥；爭吵
61 exhort [ɪgˈzɔːrt] (v.) 力勸
62 plead [pliːd] (v.) 抗辯

🎧21 On the other hand was to be seen Lady Montague pleading for her child's life, and arguing with some justice that Romeo had done nothing worthy of punishment in taking the life of Tybalt, which was already forfeited to the law by his having slain Mercutio.

The prince, unmoved by the passionate exclamations of these women, on a careful examination of the facts, pronounced his sentence, and by that sentence Romeo was banished[63] from Verona.

Heavy news to young Juliet, who had been but a few hours a bride, and now by this decree[64] seemed everlastingly divorced! When the tidings reached her, she at first gave way to rage against Romeo, who had slain her dear cousin.

She called him a beautiful tyrant, a fiend[65] angelical, a ravenous dove, a lamb with a wolf's nature, a serpent-heart hid with a flowering face, and other like contradictory names, which denoted[66] the struggles in her mind between her love and her resentment.

---

63 banish ['bænɪʃ] (v.) 放逐；驅逐出境
64 decree [dɪ'kriː] (n.) 法令；政令
65 fiend [fiːnd] (n.) 窮凶惡極的人
66 denote [dɪ'nout] (v.) 指出；指示

 But in the end love got the mastery, and the tears which she shed for grief that Romeo had slain her cousin, turned to drops of joy that her husband lived whom Tybalt would have slain. Then came fresh tears, and they were altogether of grief for Romeo's banishment. That word was more terrible to her than the death of many Tybalts.

Romeo, after the fray, had taken refuge in Friar Lawrence's cell, where he was first made acquainted with the prince's sentence, which seemed to him far more terrible than death. To him it appeared there was no world out of Verona's walls, no living out of the sight of Juliet. Heaven was there where Juliet lived, and all beyond was purgatory[67], torture, hell.

67 purgatory [ˈpɜːrɡətɔːri] (n.) 煉獄

🎧23 The good friar would have applied the consolation of philosophy to his griefs; but this frantic[68] young man would hear of none, but like a madman he tore his hair and threw himself all along upon the ground, as he said, to take the measure of his grave. From this unseemly state he was roused by a message from his dear lady, which a little revived him; and then the friar took the advantage to expostulate with him on the unmanly weakness which he had shown.

68 frantic ['fræntɪk] (a.) 狂亂的

🎧24   He had slain Tybalt, but would he also slay himself, slay his dear lady, who lived but in his life? The noble form of man, he said, was but a shape of wax when it wanted the courage which should keep it firm. The law had been lenient[69] to him, that instead of death, which he had incurred[70], had pronounced by the prince's mouth only banishment. He had slain Tybalt, but Tybalt would have slain him: there was a sort of happiness in that. Juliet was alive, and (beyond all hope) had become his dear wife; therein he was most happy.

  All these blessings, as the friar made them out to be, did Romeo put from him like a sullen[71] misbehaved wench[72]. And the friar bade him beware, for such as despaired (he said) died miserable.

---

69 lenient ['liːniənt] (a.) 寬大的；仁慈的
70 incur [ɪn'kɜːr] (v.) 招致；蒙受
71 sullen ['sʌlən] (a.) 繃著臉的；慍怒的
72 wench [wentʃ] (n.) 少婦

JULIET.   Then, window, let day in, and let life out.

ROMEO.   Farewell, farewell! one kiss, and I'll descend.

🎧 25 Then when Romeo was a little calmed, he counseled him that he should go that night and secretly take his leave of Juliet, and thence[73] proceed straightways to Mantua, at which place he should sojourn[74], till the friar found fit occasion to publish his marriage, which might be a joyful means of reconciling[75] their families; and then he did not doubt but the prince would be moved to pardon him, and he would return with twenty times more joy than he went forth with grief.

Romeo was convinced by these wise counsels of the friar, and took his leave to go and seek his lady, proposing to stay with her that night, and by daybreak pursue his journey alone to Mantua; to which place the good friar promised to send him letters from time to time, acquainting him with the state of affairs at home.

That night Romeo passed with his dear wife, gaining secret admission to her chamber, from the orchard in which he had heard her confession of love the night before. That had been a night of unmixed joy and rapture; but the pleasures of this night, and the delight which these lovers took in each other's society, were sadly allayed with the prospect of parting, and the fatal adventures of the past day.

---

73 thence [ðens] (adv.) 由彼處
74 sojourn ['soudʒɜːrn] (v.) 逗留；寄居
75 reconciling ['rekənsaɪlɪŋ] (n.) 和解

🎧26 The unwelcome daybreak seemed to come too soon, and when Juliet heard the morning song of the lark, she would have persuaded herself that it was the nightingale, which sings by night; but it was too truly the lark which sang, and a discordant[76] and unpleasing note it seemed to her, and the streaks[77] of day in the east too certainly pointed out that it was time for these lovers to part.

Romeo took his leave of his dear wife with a heavy heart, promising to write to her from Mantua every hour in the day; and when he had descended from her chamber-window, as he stood below her on the ground, in that sad foreboding state of mind in which she was, he appeared to her eyes as one dead in the bottom of a tomb. Romeo's mind misgave[78] him in like manner. But now he was forced hastily to depart, for it was death for him to be found within the walls of Verona after daybreak.

76 discordant [dɪsˈkɔːrdənt] (a.) 不和諧的
77 streak [striːk] (n.) 條紋
78 misgive [mɪsˈgɪv] (v.) 使擔心不安

27 This was but the beginning of the tragedy of this pair of star-crossed lovers. Romeo had not been gone many days before the old Lord Capulet proposed a match for Juliet. The husband he had chosen for her, not dreaming that she was married already, was Count Paris, a gallant[79], young, and noble gentleman, no unworthy suitor to the young Juliet, if she had never seen Romeo.

The terrified Juliet was in a sad perplexity[80] at her father's offer. She pleaded her youth unsuitable to marriage, the recent death of Tybalt, which had left her spirits too weak to meet a husband with any face of joy, and how indecorous[81] it would show for the family of the Capulets to be celebrating a nuptial[82] feast, when his funeral solemnities were hardly over. She pleaded every reason against the match, but the true one, namely, that she was married already.

---

79 gallant ['gælənt] (a.) 英勇的
80 perplexity [pər'pleksɪti] (n.) 困惑
81 indecorous [ɪn'dekərəs] (a.) 不合禮節的
82 nuptial ['nʌpʃəl] (n.) 結婚；婚禮

Act 3. Scene 5.

LADY CAPULET. Fie, fie! what, are you mad?
JULIET. Good father, I beseech you on my knees,
Hear me with patience but to speak a word.

🎧 28 But Lord Capulet was deaf to all her excuses, and in a peremptory[83] manner ordered her to get ready, for by the following Thursday she should be married to Paris. And having found her a husband, rich, young and noble, such as the proudest maid in Verona might joyfully accept, he could not bear that out of an affected coyness, as he construed[84] her denial, she should oppose obstacles to her own good fortune.

83 peremptory [pə'remptəri] (a.) 專橫的；獨斷的
84 construe [kən'struː] (v.) 解釋；理解為

🎧29 In this extremity Juliet applied to the friendly friar, always her counselor in distress, and he asking her if she had resolution to undertake a desperate remedy, and she answering that she would go into the grave alive rather than marry Paris, her own dear husband living; he directed her to go home, and appear merry, and give her consent to marry Paris, according to her father's desire, and on the next night, which was the night before the marriage, to drink off the contents of a phial[85] which he then gave her, the effect of which would be that for two-and-forty hours after drinking it she should appear cold and lifeless; and when the bridegroom came to fetch her in the morning, he would find her to appearance dead; that then she would be borne, as the manner in that country was, uncovered on a bier[86], to be buried in the family vault[87]; that if she could put off womanish fear, and consent to this terrible trial, in forty-two hours after swallowing the liquid (such was its certain operation) she would be sure to awake, as from a dream; and before she should awake, he would let her husband know their drift, and he should come in the night, and bear her thence to Mantua.

---

85 phial ['faɪəl] (n.) 小瓶藥水
86 bier [bɪr] (n.) 棺架；屍架
87 vault [vɑːlt] (n.) 墓穴

Love, and the dread of marrying Paris, gave young Juliet strength to undertake this horrible adventure; and she took the phial of the friar, promising to observe his directions.

Going from the monastery, she met the young Count Paris, and, modestly dissembling, promised to become his bride. This was joyful news to the Lord Capulet and his wife. It seemed to put youth into the old man; and Juliet, who had displeased him exceedingly, by her refusal of the count, was his darling again, now she promised to be obedient.

All things in the house were in a bustle[88] against the approaching nuptials. No cost was spared to prepare such festival rejoicings as Verona had never before witnessed.

On the Wednesday night Juliet drank off the potion. She had many misgivings lest the friar, to avoid the blame which might be imputed to him for marrying her to Romeo, had given her poison; but then he was always known for a holy man.

---

88 bustle ['bʌsəl] (n.) 慌忙

Act 4. Scene 3.

🎧31 Then lest she should awake before the time that Romeo was to come for her; whether the terror of the place, a vault full of dead Capulets' bones, and where Tybalt, all bloody, lay festering[89] in his shroud[90], would not be enough to drive her distracted. Again she thought of all the stories she had heard of spirits haunting the places where their bodies were bestowed. But then her love for Romeo, and her aversion[91] for Paris returned, and she desperately swallowed the draught[92], and became insensible.

89 fester ['fɛstər] (v.) 傷口化膿潰爛
90 shroud [ʃraʊd] (n.) 壽衣
91 aversion [ə'vɜːrʒən] (n.) 嫌惡
92 draught [dræft] (n.) 一飲（之量）

When young Paris came early in the morning with music to awaken his bride, instead of a living Juliet, her chamber presented the dreary spectacle of a lifeless corse[93].

What death to his hopes! What confusion then reigned through the whole house! Poor Paris lamenting his bride, whom most detestable[94] death had beguiled[95] him of, had divorced from him even before their hands were joined.

But still more piteous it was to hear the mournings of the old Lord and Lady Capulet, who having but this one, one poor loving child to rejoice and solace[96] in, cruel death had snatched[97] her from their sight, just as these careful parents were on the point of seeing her advanced (as they thought) by a promising and advantageous match.

---

93 corse [kɔːrs] (n.) 〔詩的用法〕屍體
94 detestable [dɪ'testəbəl] (a.) 可恨的
95 beguile [bɪ'gaɪl] (v.) 欺騙
96 solace ['sɑːlɪs] (v.) 安慰
97 snatch [snætʃ] (v.) 攫取

NURSE.   O lamentable day!
LADY CAPULET.   O woeful time!
CAPULET.   Death, that hath ta'en her hence to make me wail,
                 Ties up my tongue, and will not let me speak.

🎧 **33** Now all things that were ordained[98] for the festival
were turned from their properties to do the office
of a black funeral. The wedding cheer served for
a sad burial feast, the bridal hymns were changed
for sullen dirges[99], the sprightly instruments to
melancholy bells, and the flowers that should have
been strewed[100] in the bride's path, now served but to
strew her corse. Now, instead of a priest to marry her,
a priest was needed to bury her; and she was borne
to church indeed, not to augment[101] the cheerful
hopes of the living, but to swell[102] the dreary numbers
of the dead.

Bad news, which always travels faster than good,
now brought the dismal[103] story of his Juliet's death
to Romeo, at Mantua, before the messenger could
arrive, who was sent from Friar Lawrence to apprise[104]
him that these were mock funerals only, and but
the shadow and representation of death, and that
his dear lady lay in the tomb but for a short while,
expecting when Romeo would come to release her
from that dreary mansion.

98 ordain [ɔːrˈdeɪn] (v.) 注定
99 dirge [dɜːrdʒ] (n.) 輓歌
100 strew [struː] (v.) 撒⋯⋯於表面上
101 augment [ˈɔːɡˌment] (v.) 增加；增大
102 swell [swel] (v.) 使增大、增厚或加強
103 dismal [ˈdɪzməl] (a.) 陰沉的
104 apprise [əˈpraɪz] (v.) 通知

🎧 34 Just before, Romeo had been unusually joyful and light-hearted. He had dreamed in the night that he was dead (a strange dream, that gave a dead man leave to think), and that his lady came and found him dead, and breathed such life with kisses in his lips, that he revived, and was an emperor!

And now that a messenger came from Verona, he thought surely it was to confirm some good news which his dreams had presaged[105]. But when the contrary to this flattering vision appeared, and that it was his lady who was dead in truth, whom he could not revive by any kisses, he ordered horses to be got ready, for he determined that night to visit Verona, and to see his lady in her tomb.

And as mischief is swift to enter into the thoughts of desperate men, he called to mind a poor apothecary[106], whose shop in Mantua he had lately passed, and from the beggarly appearance of the man, who seemed famished, and the wretched show in his show of empty boxes ranged on dirty shelves, and other tokens[107] of extreme wretchedness, he had said at the time (perhaps having some misgivings that his own disastrous life might haply meet with a conclusion so desperate):

---

105 presage ['presɪdʒ] (v.) 預言
106 apothecary [ə'pɑːθɪkeri] (n.) 藥劑師；藥材商
107 token ['toukən] (n.) 象徵

Act. 5 Scene. 1

APOTHECARY.   Who calls so loud?
ROMEO.   Come hither, man.

35 "If a man were to need poison, which by the law of Mantua it is death to sell, here lives a poor wretch who would sell it him."

These words of his now came into his mind, and he sought out the apothecary, who after some pretended scruples[108], Romeo offering him gold, which his poverty could not resist, sold him a poison, which, if he swallowed, he told him, if he had the strength of twenty men, would quickly despatch him.

---

108 scruple ['skruːpəl] (n.) 良心不安

🎧36   With this poison he set out for Verona, to have a
sight of his dear lady in her tomb, meaning, when he
had satisfied his sight, to swallow the poison, and be
buried by her side.

He reached Verona at midnight, and found the
churchyard, in the midst of which was situated the
ancient tomb of the Capulets. He had provided a
light, and a spade, and wrenching iron, and was
proceeding to break open the monument, when he
was interrupted by a voice, which by the name of
vile Montague, bade him desist[109] from his unlawful
business.

It was the young Count Paris, who had come to the
tomb of Juliet at that unseasonable time of night, to
strew flowers and to weep over the grave of her that
should have been his bride. He knew not what an
interest Romeo had in the dead, but knowing him to
be a Montague, and (as he supposed) a sworn foe to
all the Capulets, he judged that he was come by night
to do some villainous shame to the dead bodies;
therefore in an angry tone he bade him desist; and as
a criminal, condemned by the laws of Verona to die if
he were found within the walls of the city, he would
have apprehended[110] him.

109 desist [dɪ'sɪst] (v.) 停止
110 apprehend [ˌæprɪ'hend] (v.) 逮捕

Romeo urged Paris to leave him, and warned him by the fate of Tybalt, who lay buried there, not to provoke his anger, or draw down another sin upon his head by forcing him to kill him.

But the count in scorn refused his warning, and laid hands on him as a felon[111], which Romeo resisting, they fought, and Paris fell.

When Romeo, by the help of a light, came to see who it was that he had slain, that it was Paris, who (he learned in his way from Mantua) should have married Juliet, he took the dead youth by the hand, as one whom misfortune had made a companion, and said that he would bury him in a triumphal grave, meaning in Juliet's grave, which he now opened.

111 felon ['fɛlən] (n.) 重罪犯

74

38 And there lay his lady, as one whom death had no power upon to change a feature or complexion, in her matchless beauty; or as if Death were amorous[112], and the lean abhorred monster kept her there for his delight; for she lay yet fresh and blooming, as she had fallen to sleep when she swallowed that benumbing[113] potion; and near her lay Tybalt in his bloody shroud, whom Romeo seeing, begged pardon of his lifeless corse, and for Juliet's sake called him *cousin*, and said that he was about to do him a favor by putting his enemy to death.

Here Romeo took his last leave of his lady's lips, kissing them; and here he shook the burden of his cross stars from his weary body, swallowing that poison which the apothecary had sold him, whose operation was fatal and real, not like that dissembling potion which Juliet had swallowed, the effect of which was now nearly expiring, and she about to awake to complain that Romeo had not kept his time, or that he had come too soon.

112 amorous [ˈæmərəs] (a.) 多情的
113 benumbing [bɪˈnʌmɪŋ] (a.) 使麻木的

🎧39   For now the hour was arrived at which the friar had promised that she should awake; and he, having learned that his letters which he had sent to Mantua, by some unlucky detention[114] of the messenger, had never reached Romeo, came himself, provided with a pickax[115] and lantern, to deliver the lady from her confinement[116]; but he was surprised to find a light already burning in the Capulets' monument, and to see swords and blood near it, and Romeo and Paris lying breathless by the monument.

   Before he could entertain a conjecture, to imagine how these fatal accidents had fallen out, Juliet awoke out of her trance[117], and seeing the friar near her, she remembered the place where she was, and the occasion of her being there, and asked for Romeo, but the friar, hearing a noise, bade her come out of that place of death, and of unnatural sleep, for a greater power than they could contradict had thwarted[118] their intents; and being frightened by the noise of people coming, he fled.

114 detention [dɪˈtenʃən] (n.) 阻止；延遲
115 pickax [ˈpɪkæks] (n.) 鶴嘴鋤；尖鋤
116 confinement [kənˈfaɪnmənt] (n.) 限制；監禁
117 trance [træns] (n.) 昏睡狀態
118 thwart [θwɔːrt] (v.) 反對；妨礙

JULIET.   This is thy sheath; there rust, and let me die.   Act. 5 Scene. 3

🎧40   But when Juliet saw the cup closed in her true
love's hands, she guessed that poison had been the
cause of his end, and she would have swallowed the
dregs[119] if any had been left, and she kissed his still
warm lips to try if any poison yet did hang upon
them; then hearing a nearer noise of people coming,
she quickly unsheathed a dagger which she wore, and
stabbing herself, died by her true Romeo's side.

119 dregs [dregz] (n.) 〔作複數形〕渣滓

The watch by this time had come up to the place. A page belonging to Count Paris, who had witnessed the fight between his master and Romeo, had given the alarm, which had spread among the citizens, who went up and down the streets of Verona confusedly exclaiming, "A Paris! a Romeo! a Juliet!" as the rumor had imperfectly reached them, till the uproar brought Lord Montague and Lord Capulet out of their beds, with the prince, to inquire into the causes of the disturbance.

The friar had been apprehended by some of the watch, coming from the churchyard, trembling, sighing, and weeping, in a suspicious manner. A great multitude being assembled at the Capulets' monument, the friar was demanded by the prince to deliver what he knew of these strange and disastrous accidents.

🎧 42 And there, in the presence of the old Lords
Montague and Capulet, he faithfully related the
story of their children's fatal love, the part he took in
promoting their marriage, in the hope in that union
to end the long quarrels between their families: how
Romeo, there dead, was husband to Juliet; and Juliet,
there dead, was Romeo's faithful wife; how before
he could find a fit opportunity to divulge[120] their
marriage, another match was projected for Juliet, who,
to avoid the crime of a second marriage, swallowed
the sleeping draught (as he advised), and all thought
her dead; how meantime he wrote to Romeo, to come
and take her thence when the force of the potion
should cease, and by what unfortunate miscarriage of
the messenger the letters never reached Romeo.

Further than this the friar could not follow the story,
nor knew more than that coming himself, to deliver
Juliet from that place of death, he found the Count
Paris and Romeo slain.

---

120 divulge [daɪˈvʌldʒ] (v.) 洩露；暴露

🎧 43

The remainder of the transactions[121] was supplied by the narration of the page who had seen Paris and Romeo fight, and by the servant who came with Romeo from Verona to whom this faithful lover had given letters to be delivered to his father in the event of his death, which made good the friar's words, confessing his marriage with Juliet, imploring the forgiveness of his parents, acknowledging the buying of the poison of the poor apothecary, and his intent in coming to the monument, to die, and lie with Juliet.

All these circumstances agreed together to clear the friar from any hand he could be supposed to have in these complicated slaughters[122], further than as the unintended consequences of his own well-meant, yet too artificial and subtle contrivances[123].

And the prince, turning to these old lords, Montague and Capulet, rebuked[124] them for their brutal and irrational enmities, and showed them what a scourge[125] heaven had laid upon such offenses, that it had found means even through the love of their children to punish their unnatural hate.

121 transaction [trænˈzækʃən] (n.) 處置
122 slaughter [ˈslɔːtər] (n.) 殺戮
123 contrivance [kənˈtraɪvəns] (n.) 想出的辦法
124 rebuke [rɪˈbjuːk] (v.) 指責;非難
125 scourge [skɜːrdʒ] (n.) 懲罰的工具

🎧44　And these old rivals, no longer enemies, agreed to bury their long strife in their children's graves; and Lord Capulet requested Lord Montague to give him his hand, calling him by the name of brother, as if in acknowledgment of the union of their families, by the marriage of the young Capulet and Montague; and saying that Lord Montague's hand (in token of reconcilement) was all he demanded for his daughter's jointure[126]. But Lord Montague said he would give him more, for he would raise her a statue of pure gold, that while Verona kept its name, no figure should be so esteemed for its richness and workmanship as that of the true and faithful Juliet. And Lord Capulet in return said that he would raise another statue to Romeo.

126 jointure [ˈdʒɔɪntʃər] (n.) 寡婦所得財產

So did these poor old lords, when it was too late, strive to outgo each other in mutual courtesies; while so deadly had been their rage and enmity in past times that nothing but the fearful overthrow of their children (poor sacrifices to their quarrels and dissensions) could remove the rooted hates and jealousies of the noble families.

Quotation
ROMEO AND JULIET

Chorus Two households, both alike in dignity,
In fair Verona, where we lay our scene,
From ancient grudge break to new mutiny,
Where civil blood makes civil hands unclean.
From forth the fatal loins of these two foes
A pair of star-cross'd lovers take their life;
Whose misadventur'd piteous overthrows
Doth with their death bury their parents' strife.
   (Prologue, 1-8)

合唱   事發名城維洛那，
榮顯相當兩家族，
舊日嫌隙起新亂，
鮮血污漬城民手。
命運注定兩仇敵，
生下可憐之戀人，
悽慘不幸之死亡，
和解交惡之雙親。
（開場詩，1-8 行）

84

Capulet Nay, sit, nay, sit, good cousin Capulet,
For you and I are past our dancing days:
How long is't now, since last yourself and I
Were in a mask? (I, v, 30-33)

柯譜雷 啊！坐，坐，好親戚，
你和我都已經跳不起來了；
還記得我們上一次戴面具跳舞是多久以前的事呢？
（第一幕，第五景，30-33 行）

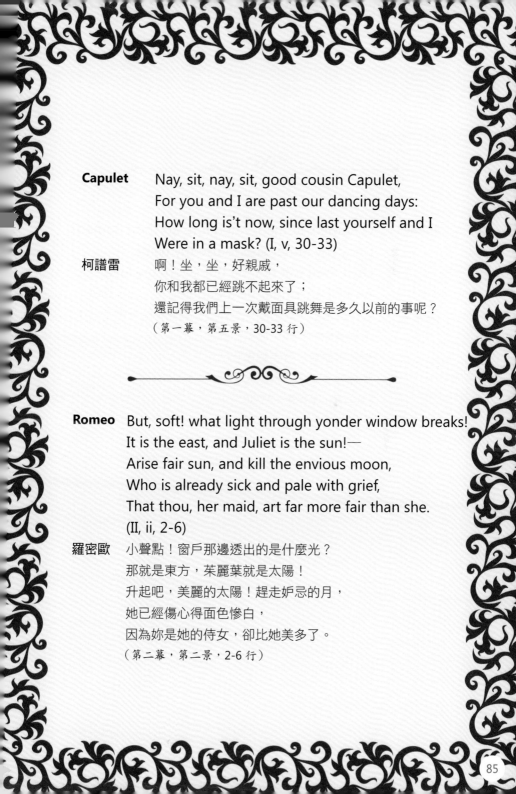

Romeo But, soft! what light through yonder window breaks!
It is the east, and Juliet is the sun!—
Arise fair sun, and kill the envious moon,
Who is already sick and pale with grief,
That thou, her maid, art far more fair than she.
(II, ii, 2-6)

羅密歐 小聲點！窗戶那邊透出的是什麼光？
那就是東方，茱麗葉就是太陽！
升起吧，美麗的太陽！趕走妒忌的月，
她已經傷心得面色慘白，
因為妳是她的侍女，卻比她美多了。
（第二幕，第二景，2-6 行）

Juliet   O Romeo, Romeo, wherefore art thou Romeo?
Deny thy father and refuse thy name;
Or, if thou wilt not, be but sworn my love,
And I'll no longer be a Capulet. (II, ii, 33-36)

茱麗葉   喔，羅密歐，羅密歐！為什麼你偏偏是羅密歐？
不要認你的父親，放棄你的姓氏吧；
你若不願意，就宣誓愛我吧，
那樣我便不再當柯家人。

（第二幕，第二景，33-36 行）

Much Ado
About Nothing

無事生非

導讀

真實生活中的喜劇

《無事生非》寫作年代應在 1598-1599 年，是莎士比亞喜劇寫作最成熟時期的創作，內容熱鬧歡樂，富有哲思。故事主旨為面具、偽裝或遊戲，劇中人物探尋的則是男女關係中的自我意識以及真誠與尊重。

在伊莉莎白時期的英國，「無事」（nothing）的發音與 noting 極為類似，因此「無事生非」也有「注意」、「紀錄」、「竊聽生非」的雙關語暗示。「竊聽」在劇中不僅常見，而且至關重要，是造成誤解或澄清事實的關鍵。

比起莎士比亞的其他喜劇，例如《連環錯》、《仲夏夜之夢》、《皆大歡喜》、《第十二夜》等，本劇的特徵是場景及語言都較為接近真實生活。《無》劇沒有脫離現實的浪漫場景，而是在梅西納城；劇中人並非一見鍾情，而是從相識的友人開始；本劇語言也不像極度浪漫的詩文，而是當時代的一般口語。諸如此類的安排，使得本劇真實性高，彷彿是一般人也會發生的故事。

劇情架構

劇中的架構主要由兩對情侶所組成。希柔和碧翠絲是情同手足的表姊妹，克勞迪和班狄克是親王唐沛左的好友，四人雙雙演出兩種截然不同的愛情。希柔優雅沉靜，克勞迪叱吒戰場，兩人代表傳統的結合。碧翠絲和班狄克之間則是永無休止的唇槍舌戰，儘管最終配對成功，但兩人都仍堅持戴著原本尖酸嘲諷的面具。

這兩條故事線，是莎士比亞取材不同故事改編而成。希柔和克勞迪的故事似乎是根據義大利的亞瑞歐托（Ariosto）1516 年出版的《憤怒的奧蘭多》（*Orlando Furioso*），以及邦代羅（Matteo Bandello）於 1554 年出版的《小說》（*Novella*）中的第二十二個短篇小說所改寫而成。這則含悲劇成分的故事，帶有浪漫多情的義大利風味。此外，在文藝復興時期，時而可見未婚女子被污衊的題材，其中也有不少以悲劇作收，史賓賽的《仙后》（*Faerie Queene*）中就有類似的例子。

碧翠絲與班狄克

碧翠絲與班狄克的故事源自英式幽默。在中古時期的英國，兩性戰爭是個常見的主題，喬叟和韋克非（Wakefield）都寫過這類故事。莎士比亞早期的《馴悍記》也是類似的題材，凱瑟琳和皮楚丘最初充滿敵意，互相羞辱和攻擊，最後卻彼此傾心。碧翠絲和班狄克的故事很成功，為英國的喜劇文學立下良好典範，王爾德和蕭伯納都是後來的佼佼者。

兩段感情的發展呈現不同的本質。碧翠絲和班狄克這兩個角色的心理層面較為複雜,他們都是自我意識很強的人,對伴侶的要求也高。然而這種生活態度往往和真實情感相左,因此需要旁人相助來讓兩人卸下高傲的面具。另外,兩人都是在偷聽到友人的談話之後才知道自己的毛病,但都誠懇地接受批評,並放下身段接受被設計而來的感情。

1861 年,白遼士將此劇改編為歌劇時,將故事改名為《碧翠絲與班狄克》(Beatrice et Benedict),無數的演員、觀眾及讀者都能認同,但兩人的戀情無法自成一個劇本,因為碧翠絲如果不要求班狄克去殺克勞迪,就無法顯示班狄克在舊友與新歡之間的為難與衝突,也無法證明他對愛情的承諾。

傳統對女性的要求

相形之下,希柔和克勞迪的故事就顯得平板單調,因而往往被視為次要角色。希柔溫馴聽話,並不像希臘神話裡的希柔,為愛打破宗教誓約,甚至犧牲性命。克勞迪對他和希柔的婚事很慎重,他請求親王作媒,在確定希柔和她父親都同意了之後才安心。這段姻緣理性而有計畫,一切遵循社會規範與門第觀念。

克勞迪冤枉希柔,看似是一場「無事生非」的誤會,但那種慘痛經驗卻是劇中人的試煉。碧翠絲和修道士深信希柔清白無辜,班狄克儘管內心掙扎,但也通過了碧翠絲的考驗。克勞迪輕易拒絕並羞辱所愛的女子,暴露了對自己和對希柔的無知,因此這場誤會並不能完全歸咎於為非作歹的唐隆。

MUCH ADO About NOTHING.

希柔的父親李歐拿多一聽到他人對女兒的指控，馬上信以為真，以為女兒做出不名譽的事，又為確保女兒對未來夫婿忠貞不二，甚至寧願她就此死去。克勞迪、親王和李歐拿多的反應，反映了男人對女人不忠的深刻恐懼。

在莎士比亞的喜劇中，幾乎都是在與死神錯身而過之後，才得到圓滿結果，例如早期的《連環錯》、《仲夏夜之夢》和後來的《皆大歡喜》等。但與《威尼斯商人》和《一報還一報》相較之下，本劇中的死亡威脅就顯得毫不緊迫。

私生子唐降和《奧塞羅》中的以阿苟一樣邪惡，善於利用人們不可靠的視覺和聽覺來誤導仇人。但他陷害希柔並不是為了求什麼好處，只不過是想惱怒親王兄長，讓親王和親王周遭的人都變得和他自己一樣陰鬱罷了。劇中對唐降這個角色的心理、性格和背景並未加以著墨，故只能說是為阻礙喜劇收場的一項安排。

人物表

Hero	希柔	和碧翠絲是表姐妹，後來與克勞迪結婚
Beatrice	碧翠絲	個性活潑，和班狄克是歡喜冤家
Leonato	李歐拿多	梅西納的總督，希柔的父親
Don Pedro	唐沛左	一位親王，想撮合碧翠絲和班狄克
Claudio	克勞迪	貴族，親王的友人
Benedick	班狄克	貴族，親王的友人
Ursula	烏蘇拉	總督的侍女
Margaret	瑪格莉特	總督的侍女
Don John	唐降	唐沛左同父異母的弟弟，想阻撓克勞迪和希柔的婚事
Borachio	包拉喬	被唐降收買，想破壞克勞迪的婚事

🎧46   There lived in the palace at Messina two ladies, whose names were Hero and Beatrice. Hero was the daughter, and Beatrice the niece, of Leonato, the governor of Messina.

   Beatrice was of a lively temper, and loved to divert[1] her cousin Hero, who was of a more serious disposition[2], with her sprightly sallies[3]. Whatever was going forward was sure to make matter of mirth[4] for the light-hearted Beatrice.

   At the time the history of these ladies commences[5] some young men of high rank in the army, as they were passing through Messina on their return from a war that was just ended, in which they bad distinguished themselves by their great bravery, came to visit Leonato. Among these were Don Pedro, the Prince of Arragon; and his friend Claudio, who was a lord of Florence; and with them came the wild and witty Benedick, and he was a lord of Padua.

---

1 divert [daɪˈvɜːrt] (v.) 娛樂；消遣
2 disposition [ˌdɪspəˈzɪʃən] (n.) 性質；氣質
3 sally [ˈsæli] (n.) 俏皮話；妙語
4 mirth [mɜːrθ] (n.) 歡樂
5 commence [kəˈmens] (v.) 開始

🎧 47   These strangers had been at Messina before, and the hospitable governor introduced them to his daughter and his niece as their old friends and acquaintance.

  Benedick, the moment he entered the room, began a lively conversation with Leonato and the prince. Beatrice, who liked not to be left out of any discourse, interrupted Benedick with saying: "I wonder that you will still be talking, Signior Benedick. Nobody marks you."

  Benedick was just such another rattlebrain[6] as Beatrice, yet he was not pleased at this free salutation, he thought it did not become a well-bred lady to be so flippant[7] with her tongue; and he remembered, when he was last at Messina, that Beatrice used to select him to make her merry jests upon.

6 rattlebrain [ˈrætlˌbreɪn] (n.) 輕率多話的人
7 flippant [ˈflɪpənt] (a.) 輕率的；無禮的

🎧 And as there is no one who so little likes to be made a jest of as those who are apt to take the same liberty themselves, so it was with Benedick and Beatrice; these two sharp wits never met in former times but a perfect war of raillery[8] was kept up between them, and they always parted mutually displeased with each other.

Therefore, when Beatrice stopped him in the middle of his discourse with telling him nobody marked what he was saying, Benedick, affecting not to have observed before that she was present, said, "What, my dear Lady Disdain, are you yet living?"

And now war broke out afresh between them, and a long jangling[9] argument ensued, during which Beatrice, although she knew he had so well approved his valor[10] in the late war, said that she would eat all he had killed there; and observing the prince take delight in Benedick's conversation, she called him "the prince's jester[11]." This sarcasm[12] sank deeper into the mind of Benedick than all Beatrice had said before.

8 raillery ['reɪləri] (n.) 善意的嘲弄
9 jangling ['dʒæŋglɪŋ] (a.) 大聲吵架的
10 valor ['vælər] (n.) 勇敢
11 jester ['dʒestər] (n.) 弄臣
12 sarcasm ['sɑːrkæzəm] (n.) 譏諷語；挖苦話

Benedick and Beatrice

🎧49 The hint she gave him that he was a coward, by saying she would eat all he had killed, he did not regard, knowing himself to be a brave man; but there is nothing that great wits so much dread as the imputation[13] of buffoonery[14], because the charge comes sometimes a little too near the truth; therefore Benedick perfectly hated Beatrice when she called him "the prince's jester."

---

13 imputation [ˌɪmpjuˈteɪʃən] (n.) 歸咎;非難
14 buffoonery [bʌˈfuːnərɪ] (n.) 滑稽;詼諧

Act. 2 Scene. 1

DON PEDRO. My visor is Philemon's roof; within the house is Jove.
HERO. Why, then, your visor should be thatched.
DON PEDRO. Speak low, if you speak love.

The modest lady Hero was silent before the noble guests; and while Claudio was attentively observing the improvement which time had made in her beauty, and was contemplating[15] the exquisite[16] graces of her fine figure (for she was an admirable young lady), the prince was highly amused with listening to the humorous dialogue between Benedick and Beatrice; and he said in a whisper to Leonato, "This is a pleasant-spirited young lady. She were an excellent wife for Benedick."

15 contemplate ['kɑːntemˌpleɪt] (v.) 注視
16 exquisite [ɪk'skwɪzɪt] (a.) 優美的

Leonato replied to this suggestion, "O, my lord, my lord, if they were but a week married, they would talk themselves mad!"

But though Leonato thought they would make a discordant pair, the prince did not give up the idea of matching these two keen wits together.

When the prince returned with Claudio from the palace, he found that the marriage he had devised between Benedick and Beatrice was not the only one projected in that good company, for Claudio spoke in such terms of Hero, as made the prince guess at what was passing in his heart; and he liked it well, and he said to Claudio, "Do you affect Hero?"

To this question Claudio replied, "O, my lord, when I was last at Messina, I looked upon her with a soldier's eye, that liked, but had no leisure for loving; but now, in this happy time of peace, thoughts of war have left their places vacant in my mind, and in their room come thronging[17] soft and delicate thoughts, all prompting me how fair young Hero is, reminding me that I liked her before I went to the wars."

17 throng [θrɔːŋ] (v.) 聚集

Hero

52 Claudio's confession of his love for Hero so wrought upon the prince, that be lost no time in soliciting[18] the consent of Leonato to accept of Claudio for a son-in-law.

Leonato agreed to this proposal, and the prince found no great difficulty in persuading the gentle Hero herself to listen to the suit of the noble Claudio, who was a lord of rare endowments[19], and highly accomplished, and Claudio, assisted by his kind prince, soon prevailed[20] upon Leonato to fix an early day for the celebration of his marriage with Hero.

Claudio was to wait but a few days before he was to be married to his fair lady; yet he complained of the interval being tedious, as indeed most young men are impatient when they are waiting for the accomplishment of any event they have set their hearts upon. The prince, therefore, to make the time seem short to him, proposed as a kind of merry pastime that they should invent some artful scheme to make Benedick and Beatrice fall in love with each other.

18 solicit [sə'lɪst] (v.) 懇求
19 endowment [ɪn'daʊmənt] (n.) 稟賦；才能
20 prevail [prɪ'veɪl] (v.) 勸說

Act 3. MUCH ADO ABOUT NOTHING. Scene I.

Beatrice

Claudio entered with great satisfaction into this whim[21] of the prince, and Leonato promised them his assistance, and even Hero said she would do any modest office to help her cousin to a good husband.

The device the prince invented was that the gentlemen should make Benedick believe that Beatrice was in love with him, and that Hero should make Beatrice believe that Benedick was in love with her.

21 whim [wɪm] (n.) 突然的念頭；一時的興致

CLAUDIO.   O, ay: stalk on, stalk on; the fowl sits. I did
            never think that lady would have loved any man.

BENEDICK.   Is't possible? Sits the wind in that corner?

🎧54 The prince, Leonato, and Claudio began their operations first; and watching upon an opportunity when Benedick was quietly seated reading in an arbor[22], the prince and his assistants took their station among the trees behind the arbor, so near that Benedick could not choose but hear all they said; and after some careless talk the prince said: "Come hither, Leonato. What was it you told me the other day—that your niece Beatrice was in love with Signior Benedick? I did never think that lady would have loved any man."

"No, nor I neither, my lord," answered Leonato. "It is most wonderful that she should so dote[23] on Benedick, whom she in all outward behavior seemed ever to dislike."

Claudio confirmed all this with saying that Hero had told him Beatrice was so in love with Benedick, that she would certainly die of grief, if he could not be brought to love her; which Leonato and Claudio seemed to agree was impossible, he having always been such a railer against all fair ladies, and in particular against Beatrice.

22 arbor [ˈɑːrbər] (n.) 涼亭
23 dote [doʊt] (v.) 鍾情

〔55〕 The prince affected to hearken[24] to all this with great compassion for Beatrice, and he said, "It were good that Benedick were told of this."

"To what end?" said Claudio; "He would but make sport of it, and torment the poor lady worse."

"And if he should," said the prince, "it were a good deed to hang him; for Beatrice is an excellent sweet lady, and exceeding wise in everything but in loving Benedick."

Then the prince motioned to his companions that they should walk on, and leave Benedick to meditate upon what he had overheard.

Benedick had been listening with great eagerness to this conversation; and he said to himself when be heard Beatrice loved him, "Is it possible? Sits the wind in that corner?"

24 hearken ['hɑːrkən] (v.) 傾聽

Benedick in the Arbor

56 And when they were gone, he began to reason in this manner with himself: "This can be no trick! They were very serious, and they have the truth from Hero, and seem to pity the lady. Love me! Why, it must be requited[25]! I did never think to marry. But when I said I should die a bachelor, I did not think I should live to be married. They say the lady is virtuous and fair. She is so. And wise in everything but loving me. Why, that is no great argument of her folly. But here comes Beatrice. By this day, she is a fair lady. I do spy some marks of love in her."

Beatrice now approached him, and said with her usual tartness[26], "Against my will I am sent to bid you come in to dinner."

Benedick, who never felt himself disposed to speak so politely to her before, replied, "Fair Beatrice, I thank you for your pains."

And when Beatrice, after two or three more rude speeches, left him, Benedick thought he observed a concealed meaning of kindness under the uncivil words she uttered, and he said aloud, "If I do not take pity on her, I am a villain. If I do not love her, I am a Jew. I will go get her picture."

25 requite [rɪ'kwaɪt] (v.) 回報
26 tartness ['tɑːrtnɪs] (n.) 尖酸；辛辣

Act. 2 Scene. 3

BEATRICE.   Against my will I am sent to bid you come in to dinner.
BENEDICK.   Fair Beatrice, I thank you for your pains.

🎧57 The gentleman being thus caught in the net they
had spread for him, it was now Hero's turn to play
her part with Beatrice; and for this purpose she sent
for Ursula and Margaret, two gentlewomen who
attended upon her, and she said to Margaret, "Good
Margaret, run to the parlor; there you will find my
cousin Beatrice talking with the prince and Claudio.
Whisper in her ear, that I and Ursula are walking in the
orchard, and that our discourse is all of her. Bid her
steal into that pleasant arbor, where honeysuckles[27],
ripened by the sun, like ungrateful minions[28], forbid
the sun to enter."

This arbor, into which Hero desired Margaret to
entice[29] Beatrice, was the very same pleasant arbor
where Benedick had so lately been an attentive
listener.

"I will make her come, I warrant, presently," said
Margaret.

---

27 honeysuckle ['hʌniˌsʌkəl] (n.) 忍冬；金銀花
28 minion ['mɪnjən] (n.) 寵僕
29 entice [ɪn'taɪs] (v.) 誘使；慫恿

Hero, then taking Ursula with her into the orchard, said to her, "Now, Ursula, when Beatrice comes, we will walk up and down this alley, and our talk must be only of Benedick, and when I name him, let it be your part to praise him more than ever man did merit. My talk to you must be how Benedick is in love with Beatrice. Now begin; for look where Beatrice like a lapwing[30] runs close by the ground, to hear our conference."

They then began, Hero saying, as if in answer to something which Ursula had said, "No, truly, Ursula. She is too disdainful; her spirits are as coy as wild birds of the rock."

"But are you sure," said Ursula, "that Benedick loves Beatrice so entirely?"

Hero replied, "So says the prince, and my lord Claudio, and they entreated me to acquaint her with it; but I persuaded them, if they loved Benedick, never to let Beatrice know of it."

---

30 lapwing ['læp,wɪŋ] (n.) 田鳧；京燕

Act. 3 Scene. 1

"Certainly," replied Ursula, "it were not good she knew his love, lest she made sport of it."

"Why, to say truth," said Hero, "I never yet saw a man, how wise soever, or noble, young, or rarely featured, but she would dispraise him."

"Sure, sure, such carping[31] is not commendable," said Ursula.

31 carp [kɑːrp] (v.) 吹毛求疵

"No," replied Hero, "but who dare tell her so? If I should speak, she would mock me into air."

"Oh, you wrong your cousin!" said Ursula, "she cannot be so much without true judgment, as to refuse so rare a gentleman as Signior Benedick."

"He hath an excellent good name," said Hero. "indeed, he is the first man in Italy, always excepting my dear Claudio."

And now, Hero giving her attendant a hint that it was time to change the discourse, Ursula said, "And when are you to be married, madam?"

Hero then told her, that she was to be married to Claudio the next day, and desired she would go in with her, and look at some new attire³², as she wished to consult with her on what she would wear on the morrow.

Beatrice, who had been listening with breathless eagerness to this dialogue, when they went away, exclaimed, "What fire is in mine ears? Can this be true? Farewell, contempt and scorn, and maiden pride, adieu! Benedick, love on! I will requite you, taming my wild heart to your loving hand."

---

32 attire [əˈtaɪr] (n.) 服裝

Beatice

It must have been a pleasant sight to see these old enemies converted[33] into new and loving friends, and to behold their first meeting after being cheated into mutual liking by the merry artifice of the good-humored prince. But a sad reverse in the fortunes of Hero must now be thought of. The morrow, which was to have been her wedding-day, brought sorrow on the heart of Hero and her good father, Leonato.

The prince had a half-brother, who came from the wars along with him to Messina. This brother (his name was Don John) was a melancholy, discontented man, whose spirits seemed to labor in the contriving of villainies.

33 convert [kənˈvɜːrt] (v.) 轉變

🎧 62 He hated the prince his brother, and he hated
Claudio, because he was the prince's friend, and
determined to prevent Claudio's marriage with Hero,
only for the malicious pleasure of making Claudio
and the prince unhappy; for he knew the prince had
set his heart upon this marriage, almost as much as
Claudio himself; and to effect this wicked purpose,
he employed one Borachio, a man as bad as himself,
whom he encouraged with the offer of a great reward.

This Borachio paid his court to Margaret, Hero's
attendant; and Don John, knowing this, prevailed
upon him to make Margaret promise to talk with him
from her lady's chamber window that night, after
Hero was asleep, and also to dress herself in Hero's
clothes, the better to deceive Claudio into the belief
that it was Hero; for that was the end he meant to
compass[34] by this wicked plot.

Don John then went to the prince and Claudio, and
told them that Hero was an imprudent lady, and that
she talked with men from her chamber window at
midnight.

34 compass ['kʌmpəs] (v.) 達到；獲得

🎧63 Now this was the evening before the wedding, and he offered to take them that night, where they should themselves hear Hero discoursing with a man from her window; and they consented to go along with him, and Claudio said, "If I see anything tonight why I should not marry her, tomorrow in the congregation[35], where I intended to wed her, there will I shame her."

The prince also said, "And as I assisted you to obtain her, I will join with you to disgrace her."

When Don John brought them near Hero's chamber that night, they saw Borachio standing under the window, and they saw Margaret looking out of Hero's window, and heard her talking with Borachio; and Margaret being dressed in the same clothes they had seen Hero wear, the prince and Claudio believed it was the lady Hero herself.

35 congregation [ˌkɑːŋerɪˈgeɪʃən] (n.) 集合

64🎧 Nothing could equal the anger of Claudio, when he had made (as be thought) this discovery. All his love for the innocent Hero was at once converted into hatred, and he resolved to expose her in the church, as he had said he would, the next day; and the prince agreed to this, thinking no punishment could be too severe for the naughty lady, who talked with a man from her window the very night before she was going to be married to the noble Claudio.

The next day, when they were all met to celebrate the marriage, and Claudio and Hero were standing before the priest, and the priest, or friar, as he was called, was proceeding to pronounce the marriage ceremony, Claudio, in the most passionate language, proclaimed the guilt of the blameless Hero, who, amazed at the strange words he uttered, said, meekly, "Is my lord well, that he does speak so wide?"

Leonato, in the utmost horror, said to the prince, "My lord, why speak not you?"

"What should I speak?" said the prince, "I stand dishonored, that have gone about to link my dear friend to an unworthy woman. Leonato, upon my honor, myself, my brother, and this grieved Claudio, did see and bear her last night at midnight talk with a man at her chamber window."

FRIAR FRANCIS. You come hither, my lord, to marry this lady.
CLAUDIO. No.
LEONATO. To be married to her: friar, you come to marry her.
FRIAR FRANCIS. Lady, you come hither to be married to this count.
HERO. I do.

Benedick in astonishment at what he heard, said, "This looks not like a nuptial."

"True, O God!" replied the heart-struck Hero; and then this hapless[36] lady sank down in a fainting fit, to all appearance dead.

The prince and Claudio left the church, without staying to see if Hero would recover, or at all regarding the distress into which they had thrown Leonato. So hard-hearted had their anger made them.

Benedick remained, and assisted Beatrice to recover Hero from her swoon[37], saying, "How does the lady?"

36 hapless ['hæpləs] (a.) 不幸的
37 swoon [swuːn] (n.) 昏厥

🎧 "Dead, I think," replied Beatrice in great agony[38] for she loved her cousin; and knowing her virtuous principles, she believed nothing of what she had heard spoken against her.

Not so the poor old father; he believed the story of his child's shame, and it was piteous to hear him lamenting over her, as she lay like one dead before him, wishing she might never more open her eyes.

But the ancient friar was a wise man, and full of observation on human nature, and he had attentively marked the lady's countenance[39] when she heard herself accused, and noted a thousand blushing shames to start into her face, and then he saw an angel-like whiteness bear away those blushes, and in her eye he saw a fire that did belie[40] the error that the prince did speak against her maiden truth, and he said to the sorrowing father, "Call me a fool; trust not my reading, nor my observation; trust not my age, my reverence, nor my calling, if this sweet lady lie not guiltless here under some biting error."

38 agony ['ægəni] (n.) 極大的痛苦
39 countenance ['kaʊntɪnəns] (n.) 面容
40 belie [bɪ'laɪ] (v.) 使人對某事得到錯誤或不實的觀念

67 When Hero had recovered from the swoon into which she had fallen, the friar said to her, "Lady, what man is he you are accused of?"

Hero replied, "They know that do accuse me; I know of none." Then turning to Leonato, she said, "O my father, if you can prove that any man has ever conversed with me at hours unmeet[41], or that I yesternight changed words with any creature, refuse me, hate me, torture me to death."

"There is," said the friar, "some strange misunderstanding in the prince and Claudio." And then he counseled Leonato, that he should report that Hero was dead; and he said that the deathlike swoon in which they had left Hero would make this easy of belief; and he also advised him that he should put on mourning, and erect a monument for her, and do all rites that appertain[42] to a burial.

"What shall become of this?" said Leonato. "What will this do?"

---

41 unmeet [ʌnˈmiːt] (a.) 不合適的
42 appertain [ˌæpərˈteɪn] (v.) 屬於

The friar replied, "This report of her death shall change slander[43] into pity; that is some good. But that is not all the good I hope for. When Claudio shall hear she died upon hearing his words, the idea of her life shall sweetly creep into his imagination. Then shall he mourn, if ever love had interest in his heart, and wish that be had not so accused her; yea, though he thought his accusation true."

Benedick now said, "Leonato, let the friar advise you; and though you know how well I love the prince and Claudio, yet on my honor I will not reveal this secret to them."

Leonato, thus persuaded, yielded; and he said sorrowfully, "I am so grieved, that the smallest twine[44] may lead me."

---

43 slander ['slændər] (n.) 誹謗；詆毀；造謠中傷
44 twine [twaɪn] (n.) 細繩

BEATRICE.   Talk with a man out at a window! A proper saying!
BENEDICK.   Nay, but, Beatrice,--

Act. 4 Scene. 1

🎧 69   The kind friar then led Leonato and Hero away to comfort and console them, and Beatrice and Benedick remained alone; and this was the meeting from which their friends, who contrived[45] the merry plot against them, expected so much diversion[46]; those friends who were now overwhelmed with affliction[47], and from whose minds all thoughts of merriment seemed forever banished.

Benedick was the first who spoke, and he said, "Lady Beatrice, have you wept all this while?"

"Yea, and I will weep a while longer," said Beatrice.

"Surely," said Benedick, "I do believe your fair cousin is wronged."

"Ah," said Beatrice, "how much might that man deserve of me who would right her!"

Benedick then said, "Is there any way to show such friendship? I do love nothing in the world so well as you. Is not that strange?"

"It were as possible," said Beatrice, "for me to say I loved nothing in the world so well as you; but believe me not, and yet I lie not. I confess nothing, nor I deny nothing. I am sorry for my cousin."

---

45 contrive [kən'traɪv] (v.) 策畫
46 diversion [daɪ'vɜːrʒən] (n.) 轉向；改道
47 affliction [ə'flɪkʃən] (n.) 痛苦；苦難

🎧 70

"By my sword," said Benedick, "you love me, and I protest I love you. Come, bid me do anything for you."

"Kill Claudio," said Beatrice.

"Ha! not for the wide world," said Benedick; for he loved his friend Claudio, and he believed he had been imposed[48] upon.

"Is not Claudio a villain, that has slandered, scorned, and dishonored my cousin?" said Beatrice, "oh, that I were a man!"

"Hear me, Beatrice!" said Benedick.

But Beatrice would hear nothing in Claudio's defense; and she continued to urge on Benedick to revenge her cousin's wrongs; and she said, "Talk with a man out of the window? a proper saying! Sweet Hero! she is wronged; she is slandered; she is undone. Oh, that I were a man for Claudio's sake! or that I had any friend, who would be a man for my sake! But valor is melted into courtesies and compliments. I cannot be a man with wishing, therefore I will die a woman with grieving."

48 impose [ɪmˈpoʊz] (v.) 利用

"Tarry[49], good Beatrice," said Benedick, "by this hand I love you."

"Use it for my love some other way than swearing by it," said Beatrice.

"Think you on your soul that Claudio has wronged Hero?" asked Benedick.

"Yea," answered Beatrice; "as sure as I have a thought, or a soul."

"Enough," said Benedick. "I am engaged; I will challenge him. I will kiss your hand, and so leave you. By this hand, Claudio shall render me a dear account! As you hear from me, so think of me. Go, comfort your cousin."

While Beatrice was thus powerfully pleading with Benedick, and working his gallant[50] temper by the spirit of her angry words, to engage in the cause of Hero, and fight even with his dear friend Claudio, Leonato was challenging the prince and Claudio to answer with their swords the injury they had done his child, who, be affirmed, had died for grief. But they respected his age and his sorrow, and they said, "Nay, do not quarrel with us, good old man."

49 tarry ['tæri] (v.) 停留
50 gallant ['gælənt] (a.) 英勇的

DON PEDRO. Runs not this speech like iron through your blood?
CLAUDIO.   I have drunk poison whiles he utter'd it.

Act. 5   Scene. 1

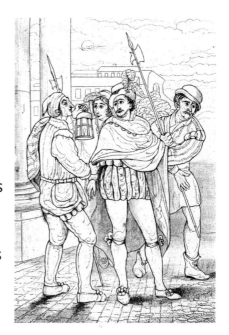

And now came Benedick, and he also challenged Claudio to answer with his sword the injury be had done to Hero; and Claudio and the prince said to each other, "Beatrice has set him on to do this."

Claudio, nevertheless, must have accepted this challenge of Benedick, had not the justice of heaven at the moment brought to pass a better proof of the innocence of Hero than the uncertain fortune of a duel.

While the prince and Claudio were yet talking of the challenge of Benedick, a magistrate[51] brought Borachio as a prisoner before the prince. Borachio had been overheard talking with one of his companions of the mischief he had been employed by Don John to do.

---

51 magistrate [ˈmædʒɪstreɪt] (n.) 地方官吏

CLAUDIO.   Is this the monument of Leonato?
LORD.   It is, my lord.
CLAUDIO.   Now, music, sound, and sing your solemn hymn.

Borachio made a full confession to the prince in Claudio's hearing, that it was Margaret dressed in her lady's clothes that he had talked with from the window, whom they had mistaken for the lady Hero herself; and no doubt continued on the minds of Claudio and the prince of the innocence of Hero. If a suspicion had remained it must have been removed by the flight of Don John, who, finding his villainies were detected, fled from Messina to avoid the just anger of his brother.

🎧74 The heart of Claudio was sorely grieved when he found he had falsely accused Hero, who, he thought, died upon hearing his cruel words; and the memory of his beloved Hero's image came over him, in the rare semblance that he loved it first; and the prince asking him if what he heard did not run like iron through his soul, he answered, that he felt as if he had taken poison while Borachio was speaking.

And the repentant Claudio implored forgiveness of the old man Leonato for the injury he had done his child, and promised, that whatever penance[52] Leonato would lay upon him for his fault in believing the false accusation against his betrothed[53] wife, for her dear sake he would endure it.

The penance Leonato enjoined[54] him was, to marry the next morning a cousin of Hero's, who, he said, was now his heir, and in person very like Hero. Claudio, regarding the solemn promise he made to Leonato, said he would marry this unknown lady, even though she were an Ethiop.

---

52 penance ['penəns] (n.) 贖罪的苦行
53 betrothed [bɪ'trouðd] (a.) 已婚的
54 enjoin [ɪn'dʒɔɪn] (v.) 命令；囑咐

🎧 75 But his heart was very sorrowful, and he passed that night in tears, and in remorseful[55] grief, at the tomb which Leonato had erected for Hero.

When the morning came, the prince accompanied Claudio to the church, where the good friar, and Leonato and his niece, were already assembled, to celebrate a second nuptial; and Leonato presented to Claudio his promised bride. And she wore a mask, that Claudio might not discover her face. And Claudio said to the lady in the mask, "Give me your hand, before this holy friar. I am your husband, if you will marry me."

"And when I lived I was your other wife," said this unknown lady; and, taking off her mask, she proved to be no niece (as was pretended), but Leonato's very daughter, the Lady Hero herself.

We may be sure that this proved a most agreeable surprise to Claudio, who thought her dead, so that he could scarcely for joy believe his eyes; and the prince, who was equally amazed at what he saw, exclaimed, "Is not this Hero, Hero that was dead?"

---

55 remorseful [rɪˈmɔːrsfəl] (a.) 極為後悔的

Hero

🎧 **76** Leonato replied, "She died, my lord, but while her slander lived."

The friar promised them an explanation of this seeming miracle, after the ceremony was ended; and was proceeding to marry them, when he was interrupted by Benedick, who desired to be married at the same time to Beatrice.

Beatrice making some demur[56] to this match, and Benedick challenging her with her love for him, which he had learned from Hero, a pleasant explanation took place; and they found they had both been tricked into a belief of love, which had never existed, and had become lovers in truth by the power of a false jest.

But the affection, which a merry invention had cheated them into, was grown too powerful to be shaken by a serious explanation; and since Benedick proposed to marry, he was resolved to think nothing to the purpose that the world could say against it; and he merrily kept up the jest, and swore to Beatrice, that he took her but for pity, and because he heard she was dying of love for him; and Beatrice protested, that she yielded but upon great persuasion, and partly to save his life, for she heard he was in a consumption.

56 demur [dɪˈmɜːr] (v.) 提出異議

CLAUDIO. And I'll be sworn upon't that he loves her;
         For here's a paper written in his hand,
         A halting sonnet of his own pure brain,
         Fashion'd to Beatrice.

Act. 5
Scene. 4

So these two mad wits were reconciled, and made a match of it, after Claudio and Hero were married; and to complete the history, Don John, the contriver of the villainy, was taken in his flight and brought back to Messina; and a brave punishment it was to this gloomy, discontented man, to see the joy and feastings which, by the disappointment of his plots, took place in the palace in Messina.

Leonato   I will be flesh and blood;
For there was never yet philosopher
That could endure the toothache patiently,
However they have writ the style of gods,
And made a pish at chance and sufferance.
(V, i, 34-38)

李歐拿多   我是個血肉之軀的凡人；
從來就沒有一個哲學家
能夠平心靜氣忍受牙痛，
儘管他們曾以神來之筆，
藐視人生的災難與痛苦。
（第五幕，第一景，34-38 行）

國家圖書館出版品預行編目資料

悅讀莎士比亞故事 .5, 羅密歐與茱麗葉 & 無事生非 /
Charles and Mary Lamb 著；Cosmos Language Workshop
　　　　譯 .
一初版 . 一 [臺北市]：寂天文化，2011.12　面；公分 .

ISBN　978-986-184-949-2 (25K 平裝附光碟片)

1. 英語 2. 讀本

805.18　　　　　　　　　　　　　　　100024158

作者	Charles and Mary Lamb
譯者	Cosmos Language Workshop
編輯	陸葵珍
主編	黃鈺云
內文排版	陸葵珍
製程管理	黃敏昭
出版者	寂天文化事業股份有限公司
電話	02-2365-9739
傳真	02-2365-9835
網址	www.icosmos.com.tw
讀者服務	onlineservice@icosmos.com.tw
出版日期	2011 年 12 月 初版一刷（250101）
	版權所有 請勿翻印
郵撥帳號	1998620-0 寂天文化事業股份有限公司
	訂購金額 600(含) 元以上郵資免費
	訂購金額 600 元以下者，請外加郵資 60 元
	〔若有破損，請寄回更換，謝謝。〕

CONTENTS

《羅密歐與茱麗葉》Practice

1 Postreading

1. Do you or your lover sometimes use literary or rhetorical devices to talk to each other as Romeo and Juliet did? Do you enjoy doing this? Why or why not?
2. What do you think about "death for love"? Give an example to support your idea.

2 Vocabulary

A. Fill in the blanks with the words from the following list.

discreet	dissensions	indecorous	provoked
nuptial	prodigious	profaned	purgatory

1. He presumed in the gentlest manner to take her by the hand, calling it a shrine, which if he _____ by touching it, he was a blushing pilgrim, and would kiss it for atonement.
2. A _____ birth of love it seemed to her, that she must love her enemy, and that her affections should settle there, where family considerations should induce her chiefly to hate.
3. The custom of _____ ladies is, to frown and be perverse, and give their suitors harsh denials at first.
4. The good friar praying the heavens to smile upon that act, and in the union of this young Montague and young Capulet to bury the old strife and long _____ of their families.
5. Mercutio looked upon his present forbearance as a sort of calm dishonorable submission, with many disdainful words _____ Tybalt to the prosecution of his first quarrel with him.
6. Heaven was there where Juliet lived, and all beyond was _____, torture, hell.

7. How _____ it would show for the family of the Capulets to be celebrating a _____ feast, when his funeral solemnities were hardly over!

B. Choose one of the following words to describe each situation.

| affect | augment | lenient | loath |

1. You are a member of a pop singer's fan club. The number of the total membership went from 8,256 last year to 10,078 now. It has been _____ed.
2. Someone in your class was caught cheating in the exam. The teacher did not fail the student but advised him not to do it again. The teacher was _____.
3. You didn't do the assignment, so you told the teacher that you were sick in order not to go to class. You _____ed sickness.
4. You and your friends were sitting in McDonald's. Someone was smoking, and all of you wanted to leave at once. You were _____ to breathe or inhale the smoke.

3 Identification: Fill in the blanks with the characters from the following list.

the apothecary	the prince
Benvolio	Juliet
old lord Capulet	Mercutio
friar Lawrence	Tybalt
count Paris	Romeo

A. Who are they?

1. _____ A friend to both the families, who joined the hands of Juliet and Romeo in marriage and counseled them in their distress.
2. _____ Son to the old lord Montague, who, secretly married to Juliet, killed Capulet's nephew and was banished from Verona.

3. _____ A friend of Romeo, who had much fire and youthful blood, was killed in a street fight.

4. _____ A nephew of lord Capulet, who was of a fiery and passionate temper and was killed by Romeo.

B.Who said or did these?

1. _____ "O Romeo, Romeo! wherefore art thou Romeo? Deny thy father, and refuse thy name, for my sake."

2. _____ "Love directed me, I am no pilot, yet wert thou as far apart from me, as that vast shore which is washed with the farthest sea, I should venture for such merchandise."

3. _____ Who was the husband that old lord Capulet had chosen for Juliet?

4. _____ Who had been eyewitness to the street fray and related the origin of it, keeping as near the truth as he could without injury to Romeo?

---

4 **Comprehension: Choose the correct answer.**

_____ 1. Who belonged to neither the Capulets nor the Montagues?
    a) Romeo.   b) Juliet.   c) Mercutio.   d) Tybalt.

_____ 2. Where did Romeo first meet Juliet?
    a) At a great supper made by old lord Capulet.
    b) In friar Lawrence's cell.
    c) In an orchard at the back of Juliet's house.
    d) In the streets of Verona.

_____ 3. Where did Juliet confess her love and exchange a vow of love with Romeo?
    a) At old lord Capulet's great supper.
    b) In friar Lawrence's monastery.
    c) At a window in the orchard at the back of her house.
    d) In the family vault of the Capulets.

_____ 4. What was the tragedy that led Romeo to banishment?
    a) A marriage of these star-crossed lovers that was not proved by their parents.

b) The old deadly enmity between the rich Capulets and the Montagues.

c) Romeo's beloved, Rosaline, showed disdain for him.

d) A street fray in which Tybalt and Mercutio were killed.

_____ 5. Which of the reasons was not Juliet's excuse for marrying Paris?

a) Her youth.

b) It was indecorous for the Capulets.

c) She was married.

d) The death of Tybalt.

_____ 6. Juliet called Romeo a beautiful tyrant, a fiend angelical, a ravenous dove, a lamb with a wolf's nature, and a serpent-heart hid with a flowering face. These are the:

a) Personification.   b) Contradictory names.

c) Mythological allusions.   d) Loving conceits.

_____ 7. Which of the following was not part of friar Lawrence's artificial and subtle contrivances?

a) Promoting Romeo and Juliet's marriage.

b) Advising Juliet to swallow the sleeping draught.

c) Writing to Romeo to come and take Juliet thence when the force of the potion should cease.

d) Urging Paris to go to the tomb of Juliet and stop Romeo.

_____ 8. What did the two rivals do after the death of Romeo and Juliet?

a) Their rage and enmity grew even higher and more serious.

b) They agreed to bury their long strife in their children's graves.

c) They strove to outdo each other in family fortunes.

d) They rebuked the friar for not having divulged his contrivances earlier.

5 Discussion

1. Discuss the language Romeo and Juliet used in the story. What rhetorical devices had they used in expressing their mutual love?
2. Discuss the two forces in conflict in this story-the dissension of the families and the young love that defies its doomed fate.
   a) How do you look at the insoluble enmity between the Montagues and the Capulets, and the street fight?
   b) How does the sudden and strong love at first sight between Romeo and Juliet, both teenagers, strive to stand among hatred?

6 Rewrite the Story

Was the death of Romeo and Juliet unavoidable to bury their parents' strife? Could you think of anything, other than friar Lawrence's contrivances, to save them from their tragedy? Write your ideas down and exchange them with your classmates.

7 Playing a Scene

Work in groups. Each group has to play one of the following scenes:

1. the dancing party at Capulet's.
2. the balcony scene.
3. the street fight scene.
4. the tomb scene.

Follow the next steps to prepare for the scene:

1. write the scene script.
2. cast the actors and actresses.
3. find the costumes that would fit the setting of your scene-either in the 16th Century Italy or in a contemporary city.
4. select some songs or music for your scene if necessary.

《羅密歐與茱麗葉》Answers

2 Vocabulary
A.
1. profaned
2. prodigious
3. discreet
4. dissensions
5. provoked
6. purgatory
7. indecorous, nuptial

B.
1. augmented
2. lenient
3. affected
4. loath

3 Identification
A.
1. friar Lawrence
2. Romeo
3. Mercutio
4. Tybalt

B.
1. Juliet
2. Romeo
3. Paris
4. Benvolio

4 Comprehension
1. c
2. a
3. c
4. d
5. c
6. b
7. d
8. b

I Postreading

1. What would you think is the main idea of this story? Is it for pure enjoyment?
2. What do you think of love when it is not out of a voluntary will (as the case of Benedick and Beatrice)? Do you have any similar experiences before?
3. Are you a sharp wit? If so, how do you feel about it? If not, What do you think of those people? Give some examples if possible.

2 Vocabulary: Fill in the blanks with the words from the following list.

soliciting	mourning	malicious	attentively
severe	sarcasm	converted	agony
erect	exquisite	account	

1. Beatrice called Benedick "the prince's jester? This _____ sunk deeper into the mind of him than all she had said before.
2. Claudio was _____ observing the improvement which time had made in her beauty and contemplating the _____ graces of her fine figure.
3. Claudio's confession of his love for Hero so wrought upon the prince, that he lost no time in _____ the consent of Leonato to accept of Claudio for a son-in-law.
4. It must have been a pleasant sight to see these old enemies _____ into new and loving friends.
5. He determined to prevent Claudio's marriage with Hero, only for the _____ pleasure of making Claudio and the prince unhappy.

6. The prince agreed to this, thinking no punishment could be too _____ for the naughty lady.

7. "Dead, I think," replied Beatrice in great _____, for she loved her cousin.

8. He also advised him that he should put on _____, and _____ a monument for her, and do all rites that appertain to a burial.

9. By this hand, Claudio shall render me a dear _____.

---

3 **Identification: Who said or did the following words and things? Choose from the list.**

Beatrice	Benedick	Borachio	Claudio
Don John	Don Pedro	Hero	Leonato
Margaret	the friar		

1. _____ "Oh, my lord, my lord, if they were but a week married, they would talk themselves mad."

2. _____ "Beatrice is an excellent sweet lady, and exceeding wise in everything but in loving Benedick."

3. _____ "If I do not take pity on her, I am a villain. If I do not love her, I am a Jew. I will go get her picture."

4. _____ "Bid her steal into that pleasant arbor, where honeysuckles, ripened by the sun, like ungrateful minions, forbid the sun to enter."

5. _____ "If I see anything tonight why I should not marry her, tomorrow in the congregation, where I intended to wed her, there will I shame her."

6. _____ "How much might that man deserve of me who would right her!"

7. _____ "Call me a fool; trust not my reading, nor my observation; trust not my age, my reverence, nor my calling, if this sweet lady lie not guiltless here under some biting error."

8. _____ Who was it that dressed in her lady's clothes that Borachio had talked with from the window?

9. _____ Who contrived the villainous scheme to deceive Claudius?

10. _____ Who was employed to deceive Claudio?

Comprehension: Choose the correct answer.

___ 1. Who are the two sharp wits in this story?
   a) Don Pedro the prince and Leonato.
   b) Claudio and Hero.
   c) Benedick and Beatrice.
   d) Borachio and Margaret.

___ 2. What made Benedick perfectly hate Beatrice?
   a) When she said that nobody marked him.
   b) When she said she would eat all he had killed in the war.
   c) When she called him "the prince's jester".
   d) When she against her will bid him come in to dinner.

___ 3. What did the prince proposed to Claudio to make the time before his marriage with Hero seem short?
   a) That they should chat among the trees behind the arbor whenever they felt tedious.
   b) That they should invent some artful scheme to make Benedick and Beatrice fall in love with each other.
   c) That they should attempt to prevent Benedick and Beatrice from any long jangling arguments.
   d) That they should solicit the consent of Leonato to accept of Benedick for a son-in-law.

___ 4. Why did the prince and Claudio mistake Margaret for Hero when she was talking with Borachio from Hero's chamber window at midnight?
   a) Because Margaret feigned Hero's voice.
   b) Because Margaret dressed herself in Hero's clothes.
   c) Because Margaret imitated Hero's gestures.
   d) Because Borachio called Margaret "Hero".

___ 5. What did Beatrice bid Benedick do for her when Hero was slandered and undone?
   a) Help her in her revenge against Hero's wrongs.
   b) Detect how this villainy was contrived.
   c) Erect a monument for Hero.
   d) Kill Claudio.

____ 6. Why was Borachio brought before the prince as a prisoner?
   a) He fled from Messina to avoid the just anger of the prince.
   b) He had been seen passing one night in remorseful grief at the tomb which Leonato had erected for Hero.
   c) He had slandered, scorned, and dishonored Hero.
   d) He had been overheard talking about the mischief he had been employed by Don John to do.

____ 7. How did Claudio spend the night before marrying Hero's "cousin"?
   a) He passed that night in tears, and in remorseful grief, at the tomb which Leonato had erected for Hero.
   b) He passed that night preparing for what would be needed for the wedding next morning.
   c) He passed that night confiding his repentance for the injury he had done Hero to the prince.
   d) He passed that night worrying that his bride would be an Ethiop.

____ 8. What did Benedick do when he found that they had both been tricked into a belief of love?
   a) He resolved to marry Beatrice and merrily kept up the jest.
   b) He furiously challenged the prince to answer with his sword the plot he had contrived.
   c) He said he never thought to marry, and that he should die a bachelor.
   d) He sunk down in a fainting fit, to all appearance dead.

5 Sequence the Story

Write down the sequences of the story. Use another sheet of paper if you need more space for details.

1. _____
2. _____
3. _____
4. _____
5. _____
6. _____
7. _____
8. _____

6 Challenge

Claudio wronged Hero because he was deceived. But it's an unbelievable deception, he must have ignored the woman's face and voice and judged only by her dress. Try to rewrite the marriage scene in which you could defend for Hero and explain Claudio's mistake. You may change the outcome accordingly.

7 Cast Your Characters

Who would you regard as the best actors and actresses to play the characters if *Much Ado about Nothing* is going to be made into a movie? Choose your favorite movie stars, singers, or the appropriate people; give sufficient reasons for your choice.

8 Act Out

Pick one of your favorite scenes of the story and act it out. Work with your partners and rehearse the scene before your presentation. Add any dialogue that you feel is needed.

《無事生非》 Answers

2 Vocabulary
A.

1. sarcasm
2. attentively, exquisite
3. soliciting
4. converted
5. malicious
6. severe
7. agony
8. mourning, erect
9. account

3 Identification
A.

1. Leonato
2. Don Pedro
3. Benedick
4. Hero
5. Claudio
6. Beatrice
7. the friar
8. Margaret
9. Don John
10. Borachio

4 Comprehension

1. c
2. c
3. b
4. b
5. d
6. d
7. a
8. a

《羅密歐與茱麗葉》中譯

P.27 富裕的柯譜雷家族和孟鐵古家族，是維洛那城的兩大望族。這兩個家族曾起齟齬，後來愈演愈烈，結下深仇大恨，最後連兩造的遠房親戚和部屬僕役都被牽連進去。孟家僕人只要碰見了柯家僕人，或是柯家人撞見了孟家人，就會互相叫罵，甚至發生喋血事件。這種一見面就吵架的情形時而可見，破壞了維洛那城街道的恬適清靜。

柯老爺舉辦一場盛宴，廣邀名媛貴客，維洛那城出名的美人都來了。只要不是孟家的人，誰來了都會受到歡迎。

P.28 羅瑟琳也來參加柯家的宴會，孟家的少爺羅密歐是她的愛慕者。宴會上要是出現孟家的人，想必會出亂子，不過好友班弗禮還是說服了羅密歐少爺戴上面具，潛進宴會，去看他的羅瑟琳。讓羅密歐看一看羅瑟琳，再跟維洛那城那些出色的美女比一比，（班弗禮說）羅密歐就會覺得他心目中的天鵝不過是隻烏鴉罷了。

羅密歐對班弗禮的話不以為然，不過因為他很喜歡羅瑟琳，所以他還是被說動了去參加宴會。羅密歐是個真摯熱情的人，他為愛失眠，常常自己一個人獨處，想的念的都是羅瑟琳。可是羅瑟琳看不上他，連報以最基本的禮貌或好意都沒有。班弗禮想帶他見識各種姑娘和朋友，讓他不要對羅瑟琳這麼痴情。

年輕的羅密歐、班弗禮和友人馬庫修，他們戴上面具來到了柯家的宴會上。柯老爺歡迎他們，告訴他們說，只要是腳上沒長繭的姑娘，誰都會想和他們跳舞。這個老人的心情很好，他還說起自己年輕的時候也會戴上面具，這樣才可以在佳人的耳邊輕聲細語地對她們說些故事。

P.30 他們跳起了舞，這時，舞池中一位美若天仙的姑娘，讓羅密歐看得目瞪口呆。羅密歐感到，因為有她的存在，火炬變得更加光輝。在這黑夜裡，她的美猶如黑人所戴上的珍貴寶石。「此美只應天上有，讓人不敢褻玩焉！」她站在眾女伴之間，（他說）就好像一隻白鴿站在烏鴉群裡，看起來是那麼閃閃動人、完美無瑕。

未料，羅密歐的喃喃讚美，被柯老爺的姪子提伯特給聽到了，提伯特認出了那是羅密歐的聲音。這個提伯特的脾氣很火爆，他不能容忍孟家人蒙面混進來嘲弄譏諷（他是這樣說的）這個隆重場合。他破口大罵，非常氣憤，恨不得一拳打死這個年輕的羅密歐。

然而提伯特的伯父柯老爺不許他當場鬧事，一來是因為考慮到其他的客人，二來也是因為羅密歐向來是個正人君子，維洛那的人們無不稱讚他是個品德好又有教養的年輕人。

P31 提伯特只好按捺住脾氣，但他發誓，改天一定要這個擅自闖入的可惡孟家人付出慘痛的代價。

跳完舞之後，羅密歐望著那位姑娘所站的地方。有了面具的掩護，羅密歐敢情放肆些。他壯起膽子，溫柔地牽起她的手，說她的手好比是神殿，而他自己是一個羞赧的朝聖者；如果他這麼一碰，褻瀆了她的手，他願意親吻它，當做贖罪。

姑娘回答：「善心的朝聖者，你的朝拜也未免太隆重多禮了。聖徒的手，朝聖者只可以摸，不可以吻。」

「聖徒和朝聖者都有嘴唇吧？」羅密歐說。

姑娘說：「有，那是做禱告用的。」

羅密歐說：「親愛的聖徒，那就請聽我的祈禱，應允我吧，不然我就會陷入絕望之地。」

P.33 這些曖昧的對話還沒說完，姑娘的母親就把她給叫走了。羅密歐打聽她母親的身分後，得知這位讓他心動不已的絕色美人，就是年輕的茱麗葉——孟家大仇人柯老爺的女兒，也是柯家的繼承人。他這下明白了自己無意間愛上了仇家的人。

他很糾結，因為他放不掉這份感情。當茱麗葉知道和她說話的是孟家的羅密歐後，也同樣忐忑不安。她和羅密歐一樣，糊里糊塗地一下子就墜入情網。這份愛情來得令她錯愕，她愛上仇家的人，而那是她的家人要她痛恨的人。

P.34 羅密歐與友人待到了半夜才離開，之後他一溜煙地就不見人影，因為他的魂留在孟家了，根本走不開。他從茱麗葉屋後的果園牆頭翻進去，想著這位新歡。不久，樓上的窗口邊出現了茱麗葉。她看起來是那麼的美，猶如東方閃爍的陽光。在旭日的耀眼光輝下，羅密歐覺得照在果園裡的微弱月光，顯得憔悴又蒼白。

她托著香腮，羅密歐巴不得自己就是她手上的手套，可以撫摸她的臉頰。她以為周遭沒人，就嘆了一口長長的氣，唉了一聲。

聽到茱麗葉的聲音，羅密歐非常興奮。他小聲地說（她沒有聽到）：「耀眼的天使，再說些話吧。妳像天使般地出現在我的上方，像長著翅膀的信使從天而降，凡人都要抬頭仰望。」

P.36 茱麗葉不察隔牆有耳，只想著今晚所邂逅的戀情。她呼喊著意中人的名字（她以為他不在場）：「哦，羅密歐！羅密歐！為什麼你偏偏是羅密歐？為了我，不要認你的父親，放棄你的姓氏吧。如果你不願意，那麼只要你發誓會永遠愛我，那我就不再當個柯家人。」

P.37 羅密歐很想回應她的這番話，但他也很想再聽她說下去。她熱情澎湃，繼續自言自語（她以為），說羅密歐不該是羅密歐，不該是孟家的人。但願他姓別的姓，要不然就把那個討厭的姓換掉，反正姓又不是長在身上的東西。只要把姓丟掉，他就可以得到她整個人了。

聽到這些深情款款的話，羅密歐再也按捺不住。他逕自接她的話，就好像她剛剛真的在對他講話一樣。他說，她要是不喜歡羅密歐這個名字，那他就不要叫羅密歐，她可以叫他「愛人」或任何什麼名字都可以，只要她喜歡就行。

P.38 聽到花園裡有男人的聲音，茱麗葉嚇了一跳。起初，她不知道半夜裡躲在暗處偷聽秘密的人是誰，但是情人的耳朵就是特別尖，雖然沒聽過羅密歐說過幾句話，可是當他再開口時，她立刻就認出了聲音的主人是年輕的羅密歐。她警告他說，孟家的人爬過果園圍牆是很危險的，萬一被她家人發現，他就死定了。

羅密歐回答：「哎呀，妳的眼睛比他們的二十把劍都還厲害。姑娘，只要妳給我一個溫柔的眼神，他們的仇恨就奈何不了我。要是不能擁有妳的愛，那我寧可死在他們的仇恨裡，也不願含恨活下去。」

「你是怎麼到這裡的？誰帶你來的？」茱麗葉問。

「是愛情帶我來的。我不會航海，但就算妳遠在天邊，為了妳，我也要冒險出海。」羅密歐回答。

P.40 茱麗葉想起剛才不小心讓羅密歐知道了自己的心意，臉頰不禁一陣緋紅，還好是在黑夜裡，羅密歐不會看到。她想收回她的話，但覆水難收。她也想謹守禮法，像個大家閨秀，和情人保持距離，然後蹙蹙眉，先讓追求者碰個大釘子，裝出一副害羞或冷漠的樣子，卻迎拒還拒。這樣，情人才不會覺得她們太容易就被追到手，畢竟，愈難得到的東西愈珍貴。

P.41 不過，她的情況容不得她又推又拒，玩玩以退為進的求偶把戲。她沒想到羅密歐會近在咫尺偷聽她的親口告白，於是她就索性坦承他剛剛所聽到的都是真心話，還稱呼他是「英俊的孟鐵古」（愛情可以把刺耳的姓變得很甜蜜）。她請他不要因為她這麼快表達愛意，就以為她很輕浮隨便，一切只能怪（如果這樣有錯的話）今晚不湊巧，不小心吐露了心意。

她還說，用一般的婦道來看，她對他的舉止也許不夠端莊，但她比那些假裝矜持覥腆而造作的人都更為真心。

P.42 羅密歐準備對天發誓，發誓自己完全不認為這樣一位貞潔姑娘會有半點不名譽之處，但她要他不要發誓。她是很喜歡他，可是她並不喜歡當晚就發誓，那樣會顯得太輕率、魯莽又突兀。

但羅密歐急著當晚就和她互定情盟，而她說，在他還沒開口要求之前，她就已經給他了。這意思是指他已經聽過她的表白，不過她想要收回那些話，重新享受對他起誓的喜悅，因為她有的是比大海還深、還浩蕩的愛。

兩人正情話綿綿時，茱麗葉被奶媽叫了進去。天都快亮了，和她同睡的奶媽覺得她該上床了。之後她又匆忙跑出來，跟羅密歐說了三、四句話。她告訴他，要是他真心愛她、有意娶她，那她明天就會派人去找他，選個黃道吉日和他結婚,她要把自己的命運交付給他,跟隨他到天涯海角。

P.44 他們在決定此事時,奶媽又叫她,她就跑進跑出,來來回回。她很捨不得放羅密歐走,就像小女孩捨不得放小鳥走一樣,小鳥才從手上跳離一會兒,就趕緊用絲線把牠拉回來。羅密歐也同樣依依不捨,對情人來說,最美的音樂就是彼此在夜裡互相傾吐的話語。

最後他們終於道別,互祝對方有個好眠。

他們分手時,東方已經泛白。羅密歐不想睡覺,他滿腦子都是情人和兩人幸福的邂逅。他沒回家,而是繞到附近的修道院去找勞倫斯修士。

這個好心修士已經起身禱告,看到年輕的羅密歐一大早就出門,就猜出他一定是因為什麼少年情懷而整夜失眠。

P.45 他是猜對了羅密歐為情一夜未眠,可是他猜錯對象了,以為他是為羅瑟琳而失眠。

當羅密歐說他剛愛上了茱麗葉,想請修士當天為他們證婚時,修士抬起雙眼、舉起雙手,對羅密歐的變心大為吃驚。修士私下明白羅密歐是如何地愛羅瑟琳,也知道他如何嘀咕她看不起他。修士於是說,年輕人不是用真心來愛,而是用眼睛來愛。

P.46 羅密歐回答,羅瑟琳並不愛他,修士不也常怪他不該對她太過癡情的嗎?而他和茱麗葉是兩情相悅。修士只好勉強接受他的理由,他心裡想,或許茱麗葉和羅密歐這對年輕人的親事,會是消除柯孟兩家多年仇恨的好方法。這位好心的修士和兩家都很要好,所以最為兩家之間的嫌隙感到惋惜。他常想調解兩家的糾紛,不過都沒有成功。他一方面因為有此打算,一方面也是因為他很疼愛年輕的羅密歐,無法拒絕他,所以這位老人家就同意為兩人主婚。

P.47 羅密歐頓時感到萬分幸福。依約派人去找羅密歐的茱麗葉知道了此事,就早早趕到了勞倫斯的修道密室,兩人就在那裡締結了神聖的婚姻。好心的修士祈禱上天能夠眷顧這樁姻緣,藉由這對孟柯兩家年輕人的結合,可以把兩家的舊仇宿怨一起埋葬。

P.49 茱麗葉在婚禮結束後就趕忙回家,焦急地等待夜晚來臨,因為羅密歐說晚上要來他們昨晚碰面的果園裡找她。這段時間對她來說真是難熬,她就像一個在盛大節日前夕感到焦躁的小孩,雖然得到了新衣服,卻要等到隔天早上才能穿。

P.50 當日約莫正午,羅密歐的友人班弗禮和馬庫修在走過維洛那城的街道時,碰上了一群柯家的人,而走在最前頭的正是火爆的提伯特。他就是那個在柯老爺的晚宴上,氣沖沖地想和羅密歐幹一架的提伯特。

提伯特一看到馬庫修,就粗魯地指責他和孟家的羅密歐往來。馬庫修和提伯特一樣脾氣暴戾、血氣方剛,他很衝地對他的指責回嘴。班弗禮竭力調解,想要平息兩人的怒氣,可是他們還是吵了起來。當羅密歐剛好經過時，凶悍的提伯特將矛頭從馬庫修轉向羅密歐，蔑稱他是「惡棍」。

羅密歐極力想避免和提伯特發生衝突，因為他是茱麗葉的親戚，茱麗葉也很喜歡他。此外，這位年輕的孟家人生性就聰明溫和，從沒捲進過這種家族爭鬥。再加上「柯譜雷」是他心愛姑娘的姓，如今這個姓氏與其說是激怒人的口令，還不如說是消除仇恨的咒語。

P.52 他設法和提伯特講道理，客氣地以「好柯譜雷」來稱呼他，儘管他是孟家的人，他在喊出這個姓氏時，暗地裡也有些喜悅。無奈提伯特恨透所有孟家的人，他拔出劍，根本不聽什麼道理。馬庫修不知道羅密歐向提伯特求和的原因，他看到他這樣吞忍，以為他怕事，想委曲求全。所以他就口出惡語，挑釁提伯特，繼續爭吵。接著，他們兩個人打了起來，羅密歐和班弗禮努力想把兩個人分開，但是都沒有成功。最後，馬庫修受到了致命的攻擊，倒地不起。

馬庫修一死，羅密歐就再也忍不住，他回敬提伯特，也蔑稱他是惡棍。他們動起手來，最後，羅密歐殺死了提伯特。

P.53 這個可怕的亂子發生在日中的維洛那城中心。消息一傳開，出事地點很快就圍來了大批的民眾，柯孟兩家的老爺和夫人都來到了現場，親王隨即也趕了過來。親王和被提伯特殺死的馬庫修是親戚，又加上他理政時常被孟柯兩家的事鬧得不得安寧，所以他下決定心一定要揪出兇手，並且嚴加懲治。

班弗禮親眼目睹了這場打鬥，親王要他陳述事情的原委。在不會不利於羅密歐的情況下，班弗禮盡可能據實以告，並盡量為羅密歐辯解，以降低羅密歐在整個事件中的參與程度。

柯夫人失去了親人提伯特，十分悲痛，一心只想報復。她請親王嚴懲兇手，不要聽信班弗禮的話，班弗禮是孟家的人，是羅密歐的朋友，説話一定會有所偏袒。就這樣，她告了自己的新女婿，雖然她還不曉得他就是她的女婿、是茱麗葉的丈夫。

P.54 另一邊，孟家夫人則為孩子的性命求情。她辯説，羅密歐不應該為殺死提伯特而受罰，因為提伯特先殺了馬庫修，犯法在先。

親王慎查事實，不被兩個激動婦人的叫喊所動搖。他宣佈判決，依判決，羅密歐將被驅逐出維洛那城。

這對年輕的茱麗葉來説，實在是個難以承受的消息。她才當了幾個鐘頭的新娘子，如今一道命令下來就要永遠分離！消息傳來時，她一開始是生羅密歐的氣，怪他殺了親愛的堂哥。

她説他是俊美的暴君、天使般的魔鬼、烏鴉般黑的鴿子、狼心的羔羊、花朵的外表下藏著蛇蠍心腸，她説著這些自相矛盾的稱呼，透露出內心的愛恨掙扎。

P.55 最後，愛情佔了上風。她因羅密歐殺死堂哥而流的傷心淚，變成了慶幸的眼淚，因為提伯特想要殺她的丈夫，而她的丈夫還活著。但後來她又哭了起來，因為傷心羅密歐要被放逐。死了好幾個提伯特的消息，都還不及「放逐」這個字眼更教她驚駭。

在那場打鬥之後，羅密歐躲進了勞倫斯的修道密室。他在密室裡得知了親王的判決，他覺得這個判決比死刑還可怕。對他來說，出了維洛那城的城牆，就沒別的世界了。要是見不到茱麗葉，那他就活不下去。有茱麗葉的地方就是天堂，否則就是煉獄、折磨、地獄。

P.56 好心的修士原本想安慰他說一切都是命中注定，切莫過於悲傷，但這個發狂的年輕人什麼也聽不下去。他像瘋子似地扯自己的頭髮，整個人癱在地上，說要量量自己的墓穴大小。後來心愛的妻子派人捎信來，他才從這種不堪的情況中振作了些。修士趁機警告他，說他剛才的軟弱德性太沒有男子氣概了。

P.57 他殺了提伯特，難道也要把自己殺掉，把和他相依為命的心愛妻子殺掉嗎？修士說，人在表面上看起來很高貴，可是要是少了堅定的勇氣，那就不過是一尊蠟像罷了。他犯的是死罪，親王卻只親口宣判驅逐他，法律對他已經很寬容了。本來是提伯特想殺他的，結果卻是他殺了提伯特，這一點也很僥倖。茱麗葉還活著，而且成為他的愛妻（誰也料想不到），就這點來看，他是最幸福的人了。

修士跟他說，他是如何如何的幸福，但羅密歐就像個乖張無禮的少女，理都不理。修士請他當心，（他說）自暴自棄讓人不得善終。

P.59 待羅密歐平靜些，修士建議他，當晚就偷偷去和茱麗葉道別，然後馬上前往曼圖亞，在那裡落腳，直到修士找到機會宣布他們已經結婚的消息，這或許會是使兩家盡棄前嫌的好方法。修士自信到時一定能說動親王赦免羅密歐，雖然羅密歐現在離開得很痛苦，但到時候他就能懷著二十倍的喜悅返鄉。

修士的策略說服了羅密歐，他告別修士去找妻子，打算當晚待在她那裡，天一亮就獨自動身前往曼圖亞。好心的修士答應不時會捎信去曼圖亞給他，讓他知道家中的情況。

當晚，羅密歐從之前半夜偷聽到茱麗葉告白的果園裡潛入閨房，和心愛的妻子共度了一夜。這一夜充滿真摯的欣喜和痴迷，但一想到即將到來的分離，一想到白天所發生的不幸事情，這一晚的喜悅和與愛人相伴的幸福，又不幸地給沖淡了。

P.60 不受歡迎的黎明似乎來得太快。茱麗葉聽到雲雀的晨鳴，她想騙自己相信那是夜鶯的夜啼。但唱歌的確是雲雀，那個聲音是那麼嘈雜難聽，而東方的曙光也無疑地指出該是戀人分手的時刻了。

羅密歐帶著沉重的心情告別愛妻，答應到了曼圖亞一定會常常寫信回來給她。他從茱麗葉房間的窗戶爬下來，站在地上抬頭望她。她心裡有著不祥的預感，所以眼前這一幕他看起來像是墓穴裡的屍首。他對她也有同樣的感受，可是他必須趕緊離開。如果他天亮後被發現還待在維洛那城內，那他就得被處死。

P.62 對這對不幸的戀人來說，悲劇才剛要開始。羅密歐走後沒有幾天，柯老爺向茱麗葉談起一門婚事。他作夢也沒想到女兒已經結婚了，他為她所挑選的丈夫是年少英勇的高貴紳士裴力司伯爵。如果年輕的茱麗葉沒有遇到羅密歐，那他倒還配得上她。

父親所提的親事讓擔驚受怕的茱麗葉非常茫然。她說，自己還太年輕，不適合結婚，提伯特又剛死不久，她提不起精神，無法高高興興地面對丈夫，況且柯家才剛辦完喪事，如果接著就舉行婚宴，會顯得很不成體統。她用各種理由來推卻婚事，就是不提真正的原因：她已經嫁作人婦。

P.63 柯老爺不理會她的理由，專橫地要她做好準備，下週四她就要嫁給裴力司。他為她找的丈夫年輕有錢又高貴，即使是維洛那城最高傲的姑娘，也會歡歡喜喜地接受這門親事。也因此，當他看到茱麗葉拒絕時，就以為她只是在故作姿態。他不容許她阻礙自己的美好未來。

P.64 茱麗葉無路可走，便跑去請教好心的修士。她有苦惱時，一向都會找修士談。修士問她是否能下決心採取孤注一擲的方法，她回答，她心愛的丈夫還活著，如果要她嫁給裴力司，那她寧可活著躺進墳墓裡。修士叫她先回家，裝出一副開心的樣子，並依父親的意思，答應嫁給裴力司。修士給她一小瓶藥水，要她在明天晚上，也就是婚禮的前一天晚上，把藥水喝下去。藥水喝下去之後的四十二小時之內，她會全身冰冷，就像死屍一樣。這樣，新郎隔天早上來迎娶她時，就會以為她已經斷氣。接著，依照地方習俗，她會被抬上棺，然後不蓋上棺蓋地運到族墳裡去下葬。修士說，要是她能克服女人家的膽怯，同意這個可怕的考驗，那麼吞下藥水四十二個小時之後，她必定醒來（確定效力會如此），這一切都只會像是一場夢而已。而在她醒來之前，他會通知她的丈夫這件事，要她丈夫在夜裡趕來，把她帶去曼圖亞。

P.65 愛情和嫁給裴力司的恐懼，讓年輕的茱麗葉有了力量去接受這件可怕的事。她接過修士的藥水，答應照他的指示去做。

她在從修道院回來的途中，碰見了年輕的裴力司伯爵，她得體地假裝答應做他的新娘子。這對柯老爺和柯夫人來說，真是個好消息，老人家們頓時又顯得喜氣洋洋。她之前拒絕伯爵的親事，柯老爺很不高興，現在聽到她願意乖乖聽話，就又寵愛起她了。

全家上上下下趕忙張羅即將到來的婚禮，為了準備一場維洛那城空前的盛大喜宴，柯家多少錢都捨得花。

週三晚上，茱麗葉把藥喝下去。她心中有許多顧慮，擔心修士會因為要逃避為她和羅密歐證婚的責任，所以拿毒藥給她吃，不過人人都知道修士是一個聖潔的人。

P.66 她又擔心，要是她醒過來時，還不見羅密歐來，那可怕的墓穴會不會把她嚇得精神錯亂？那裡躺著的都是柯家人的屍骨，而且還躺著渾身是血、在壽衣裡逐漸腐爛的提伯特，她想起了以前聽過的那些靈魂留連停屍處的故事。接著她又想起對羅密歐的愛和對裴力司的嫌惡，才不顧一切把藥水一口吞下去，隨後失去了知覺。

P.67 一早，年輕的裴力司帶著樂隊前來喚醒新娘，可是他沒有看到活生生的茱麗葉，只看到房間裡一片死寂，躺著一具冰冷的屍體。

裴力司的期待如此落空！屋裡上上下下一片混亂！可憐的裴力司為他的新娘痛哭，可恨的死神把他的新娘拐走，在還沒成親之前就拆散他們。

柯老爺和柯夫人的哀號更是令人不忍聽聞，他們膝下就只有這個孩子，就只有這麼一個可憐的孩子可以帶給他們快樂和安慰。就在這兩位設想周到的父母眼見這一門親事即將要送她飛上枝頭時（他們以為），無情的死神卻從他們眼前把她給帶走。

P.69 現在，為婚禮所匆忙準備的一切，變成哀戚喪事之用。婚禮喜宴變成喪禮筵席，婚禮的詩歌改成悲傷的輓歌，輕快的樂器換成沈鬱的喪鐘，要用來撒在新娘走道上的鮮花，如今用來撒在屍體上。不需要牧師為她證婚，而是需要牧師為她主持葬禮。她是被帶進教堂，但這並沒有為活著的人增添愉快的希望，而是不幸地又多了一位死者。

勞倫斯修士派人去通知羅密歐這是一場假葬禮，他的愛妻只是表面上詐死，暫時躺在墳墓裡，等著他去陰森的巨室裡把她救出來。但壞消息總是傳得比好消息快，修士派去的人都還沒趕到曼圖亞，茱麗葉的死亡噩耗就已經傳到了羅密歐的耳裡。

P.70 在這之前，羅密歐還一直很雀躍快活。他夜裡夢見自己死了（這夢真奇怪，死了的人還能思考），妻子來找他，她看到他死了就親吻他，把氣吹進他的唇間，結果他竟然復活，而且還當上了皇帝！

這時有人從維洛那城送信來，他想一定會如夢兆所示，送來什麼好消息。然而，消息卻偏偏和他的美夢相反，真正死掉的是妻子，而且他再怎麼親吻她，她也不會復活了。他立刻叫人備馬，決定當晚回維洛那城，去妻子的墳墓裡看她。

人在絕望之際，很容易產生不好的念頭。他想起曼圖亞有個窮藥師，他日前才打從他的店門口經過。藥師的外表看起來像要飯的，一副餓相，店裡的骯髒架子上所放的空罐子等各種東西，都讓他看起來很寒愴潦倒。他當時說（也許擔心他的悲慘生活到頭來要鋌而走險）：

P.71 「依曼圖亞的法律，賣毒藥是死罪，可是如果有人需要，這裡有個可憐蟲可以賣給他。」

羅密歐想起他的這句話，便前去找他。藥師假裝有所遲疑，但等羅密

21

歐掏出錢後，貧窮就不容他抵抗了。他把毒藥賣給羅密歐，告訴他只要吞下毒藥，哪怕他擁有二十個男人的氣力，照樣馬上斃命。

P.73 羅密歐帶上毒藥朝著維洛那城前進，準備去愛妻的墳墓裡見妻子。換句話說，等他把妻子看個夠了以後，他就要吞下毒藥，和妻子葬在一塊。

他在半夜時抵達維洛那。他找到教堂墓園，墓園的正中央就是柯家的族墳。他拿出燭火、鏟子和鐵鍬，就在他正要撬開墓門時，一個聲音打斷了他。這個聲音稱他是可惡的孟鐵古，要他住手，不要做不法之事。

這個人是年輕的裴力司伯爵。在半夜這個不當的時刻裡，他來茱麗葉的墳上獻花、哭泣，因為她本來應該已經是他的新娘子了。他不知道羅密歐對死者有什麼企圖，只曉得他是孟家的人，（他以為）是所有柯家人的死敵。他以為羅密歐三更半夜跑來，一定是想要侮辱死者的屍體，所以生氣地叫他住手。況且羅密歐還是個罪犯，依維洛那的法律，只要他在城裡被逮著，就是死罪，裴力司因此要逮捕他。

P.74 羅密歐要裴力司走開，否則下場就會和葬在這個墳墓裡的提伯特一樣。他警告裴力司不要惹他，逼他殺他，在他身上多犯下一條罪。

伯爵不屑他的警告，只當他是重犯，動手要抓他，兩人於是打了起來。最後，裴力司倒地不起。

羅密歐走近裴力司，用火把的光一看，才知道他殺的人正是原來要娶茱麗葉的人（他由曼圖亞回來的途中知道了這件事）。厄運彷彿讓羅密歐和裴力司作了伴，羅密歐拉起這個斷氣年輕人的手，說要把他葬在勝利的墳墓裡，也就是茱麗葉的墳墓。

P.75 羅密歐打開墳墓，墳裡躺著他的妻子。她仍舊美麗無比，看來，死神一點也沒辦法讓她的容貌或膚色變樣。或者說，瘦巴巴、令人厭惡的死神也愛上了她，所以把她留在墓裡讓自己高興。她躺在那裡，依舊那麼嬌嫩明艷，她的樣子就跟她剛吞下麻醉藥後睡去一樣。她的身旁躺著壽衣沾滿血漬的提伯特，羅密歐一看到提伯特的屍體，就對著屍體請求原諒。因為茱麗葉的緣故，他稱提伯特為「堂哥」，還說要幫他個忙：殺掉他的仇人。

在此，羅密歐親吻妻子的雙唇以做為訣別。他吞下藥師賣給他的毒藥，好把厄運重擔從疲憊的身體給擺脫掉。和茱麗葉服下的假毒藥不一樣，羅密歐的毒藥會叫人送命。茱麗葉的劑藥逐漸失去藥效，她即將甦醒過來，然後抱怨羅密歐不守時──或是說他來得太早了。

P.76 已經到了修士保證她會醒過來的時間了。修士剛得知，因為一些事不湊巧，他派去曼圖亞的信差在路上給耽擱了，始終未能把信送到羅密歐的手裡。修士於是帶著尖鋤和燈籠趕來，準備把關在墳裡的茱麗葉救出來。當他看到柯家墓裡透出燈火時，他吃了一驚。隨後，他看到附近有劍和血跡，俱已斷氣的羅密歐和裴力司則躺在墓旁。

在他還來不及思考和推測這些不幸的事情是如何發生時，茱麗葉在昏迷中甦醒了過來。她看到一旁的修士後，才想起自己怎麼會來到這個地方。她問起羅密歐，但修士聽到一陣噪音，就叫她不要再繼續這種非自然的睡眠，趕緊離開這個死者之地，因為擋不住的力量就要來阻礙他們的計畫了。修士聽到有人走近，便落荒而逃。

P.77 茱麗葉看到她心愛的情人手裡握著杯子，猜他是服毒而亡。要是杯中還留有殘藥，她一定也會把它吞下去的。她吻著他那還有餘溫的雙唇，想嚐他唇上所可能殘留的毒藥。隨後，她聽到眾人走近的聲音，便迅速拔出自己隨身佩帶的短劍，然後往自己身上刺下去，倒在她忠誠的羅密歐身邊。

P.78 這時趕來了守衛。裴力司伯爵的僮僕看到主人和羅密歐在打鬥，就急急跑去找人來幫忙。城民們在維洛那的街道上奔相走告，因為聽到的傳言片斷不全，所以有人嚷著「裴力司！」，有人喊著「羅密歐！」，有人叫著「茱麗葉！」，一片混亂。隨後，孟老爺和柯老爺也被這場騷動吵醒，跟著親王一起前來探個究竟。

守衛們抓到了修士。因為修士從教堂墓園那邊走過來，他打著哆嗦、嘆著氣，還流著眼淚，令人起疑。大批人群圍聚在柯家族墓旁，對於這件離奇的慘劇，親王要修士把他知道的事都說出來。

P.80 修士當著孟老爺和柯老爺的面，詳實述說兩個孩子之間的生死戀，並表示自己促成了他們的婚事，目的是希望兩人的婚姻可以結束兩家長久以來的爭執。他說，躺在那裡的羅密歐是茱麗葉的丈夫，躺在那裡的茱麗葉是羅密歐忠貞的妻子。他還沒找適當機會宣佈兩人的婚姻時，就有人來向茱麗葉提親。為了避免犯重婚罪，茱麗葉就（依他的建議）吞下安眠藥詐死。期間，他寫信給羅密歐，要他在藥效消退的時候把茱麗葉帶走，但信差不幸誤事，羅密歐始終沒有收到信。

接下來發生的事情修士就不知道了，只知道自己來這裡要把茱麗葉從墓穴裡救出去，卻看到裴力司伯爵和羅密歐都已經斷氣。

P.81 看到裴力司和羅密歐在打鬥的僮僕，以及同羅密歐從維洛那前來的僕人，為剩下的經過做了補充說明。忠實情人羅密歐把要給父親的信，託僕人在他死後送過去，而這封信也證實了好心修士的供詞。信中，羅密歐說自己和茱麗葉結了婚，請求父母諒解；他也提到他向窮藥師買毒藥，打算去墓裡尋死，和茱麗葉躺在一起。

這些細節之間沒有出入，修士就沒有了參與這場複雜凶殺案的嫌疑。他原是一番好意，卻因為方法太過詭譎造作，而導致了這些始料未及的結果。

親王轉身向柯孟兩位老爺，指責他們不該懷著殘暴又荒謬的仇恨，表示上帝因此給了他們的過錯這等懲罰，甚至藉由子女的一場戀愛來處罰他們這種人為的仇恨。

P.82 兩家世仇於是同意把宿怨都埋進孩子的墳墓裡，從此不再敵對。柯老

23

爺請孟老爺把手給他，稱他為大哥，看似是承認了柯孟兩家年輕人的婚姻，讓他們成了親家。他說，他為女兒所要求的所有贍養就是孟老爺的手（以作為和好的象徵），但孟老爺說他要付更多的贍養費，為她鑄一尊純金雕像，只要維洛那城名聲不墜，忠貞茱麗葉的雕像就會是天下最華麗精緻的雕像。柯老爺接著表示，他也要鑄一尊羅密歐的雕像。

P.83 當事情已經無可挽回時，這兩個可憐的老家長才爭著對彼此示好。他們舊日的仇恨怨氣那麼深，只有經過子女可怕的死亡（是他們爭執不和之下的可憐犧牲品），才消除了這兩家貴族之間根深柢固的仇恨。

P.96 梅西納皇宮裡住了兩位姑娘，一位叫希柔，一位叫碧翠絲。希柔是梅西納總督李歐拿多的女兒，碧翠絲是他的姪女。

碧翠絲個性活潑，希柔天性較為嚴肅，碧翠絲就喜歡說些俏皮話來逗逗表妹。不管是什麼事情，輕鬆自在的碧翠絲總能拿來消遣一番。

這兩位姑娘的故事是這樣開始的：軍隊裡幾個高官階的年輕人，他們驍勇善戰，剛結束戰役返國，在路過梅西納時特地前來拜訪李歐拿多。他們當中有葉落崗的親王唐沛左，有親王的友人克勞迪（弗羅倫斯的貴族），與他們同來的還有機智而不拘小節的班狄克（帕都亞的貴族）。

P.97 這些訪客以前就來過梅西納，好客的總督待他們如老友舊識，把自己的女兒和姪女介紹給他們。

班狄克一進屋裡，就熱絡地和李歐拿多和親王聊了起來。不喜歡被排除在談話之外的碧翠絲，打斷班狄克說：「班狄克先生，我倒奇怪你怎麼還在講話，又沒有人理你。」

儘管班狄克和碧翠絲一樣輕率多話，但班狄克還是不滿她那種隨隨便便的問候方式。他想，這麼出言不遜的姑娘，想必不是很有教養。他還記得上次在梅西納時，碧翠絲就老愛拿他開玩笑。

P.99 喜歡開別人玩笑的人，反而不喜歡別人拿他來開玩笑，班狄克和碧翠絲就是這樣的人。這兩個機智風趣的人以前只要一見面，就會你來我往，唇槍舌戰一番，然後搞得不歡而散。

他現在話說到一半，就被碧翠絲打斷，還說什麼沒有人在聽他說話。班狄克於是故意假裝沒有注意到她在場，說道：「什麼！親愛的傲慢小姐，妳還活著啊？」

剎時他們又展開舌戰。碧翠絲說她要把他在沙場上所殺的人都吃掉，儘管她知道班狄克在這次的戰役中表現英勇。她又注意到親王很喜歡聽班狄克說話，所以稱他是「親王的弄臣」，這個嘲諷比其他的挖苦話都更讓班狄克覺得刺耳。

P.100 她借由說要吃光他所殺掉的人，來暗指他是懦夫，但他自視為勇者，這種話他才不在乎。然而，一個機智聰明的人就怕被說成是小丑，因為這種指責有時會太過接近事實。聽到碧翠絲說他是「親王的弄臣」，班狄克氣得牙癢癢。

P.101 在貴客的面前，個性謹慎的希柔默不作聲。克勞迪留意到她人長得愈來愈標緻，他注視著她婀娜多姿的身材（她本來就是個容易令人傾心的姑娘）。親王興致高昂地聽著班狄克和碧翠絲的有趣鬥嘴，他小聲地對李歐拿多說：「這個姑娘性情活潑開朗，給班狄克當妻子一定是絕配。」

P.102 聽到這項提議，李歐拿多答道：「啊，殿下呀，殿下呀，他們要是結婚，兩個人不出一個星期就會吵瘋的。」

儘管李歐拿多認為兩人不配，可是親王並沒有放棄撮合這兩個智多星的念頭。

克勞迪陪伴親王從王宮裡回來。親王發現，他們一路上不只談到撮合班狄克和碧翠絲這事，克勞迪還談到了希柔。聽他談希柔的樣子，親王猜到了他的心思。親王樂見其成，便對克勞迪說：「妳喜歡希柔？」

克勞迪回答說：「喔，殿下，我上次在梅西納時，是用軍人的心態來看待她，我心裡頭雖然喜歡她，但沒有時間談戀愛。現在，天下清平和樂，毋需掛念戰事，所以就想到了男女之事。腦海裡希柔的倩影，讓我想起在出征之前就有的情意。」

P.104 聽到克勞迪表白對希柔的感情，親王很感動。他半刻也沒耽誤，就請求李歐拿多同意將克勞迪納為女婿。

李歐拿多贊成了這門親事，親王也沒費多大功夫，就說服溫柔的希柔親自接受高貴的克勞迪的求婚。克勞迪一表人材，功業有成，又有好心親王幫忙撮合，很快就說動李歐拿多盡早擇日幫他們舉行婚禮。

再過幾天，克勞迪就可以迎娶他的美麗女郎，但在這之前卻顯百聊賴。的確，不管是什麼事情，大多數的小伙子在專心期待某件事情完成之際，總會有幾許的不耐煩。親王為了排遣克勞迪的時間，就提出一個有趣的樂子：想個妙計把班狄克和碧翠絲送作堆。

P.105 克勞迪興奮地參與了親王的這個突發奇想，李歐拿多也答應要一起通力合作，連希柔都說她願意盡棉薄之力，幫表姊找到一個好丈夫。

親王想到的點子是，男士們去讓班狄克相信碧翠絲迷戀他，希柔則去讓碧翠絲相信班狄克愛上了她。

P.107 親王、李歐拿多和克勞迪率先行動。他們等待時機，在班狄克安靜坐在涼亭裡看書時，親王和幫手們就站在涼亭後面的樹叢裡。他們故意離班狄克很近，讓他不得不聽到他們的談話。一陣閒聊之後，親王說：「李歐拿多，快過來。你那天是告訴我什麼啊，你說你的姪女碧翠絲愛上了班狄克先生？我萬萬也沒想到那位姑娘會愛上男人呀。」

「是啊，殿下，我也沒想到。」李歐拿多回答：「最妙的是她竟會喜歡上班狄克，她表面上看起來和他很不合。」

為了引證自己所說的話，克勞迪還說這是希柔告訴他的，說碧翠絲很迷戀班狄克，要是班狄克拒絕她，她一定會傷心而死。然而，李歐拿多和克勞迪都覺得他是不可能愛她的，因為班狄克一向喜歡嘲弄美女，尤其是嘲弄碧翠絲。

P.108 親王一邊聽，一邊裝出一副很同情碧翠絲的樣子。他說：「要是有人告訴班狄克這件事就好了。」

「那有什麼用？班狄克會拿這事來消遣的，這只會讓可憐的姑娘更加難過罷了。」克勞迪說。

親王說：「班狄克要是敢這樣，應該要把他絞死。碧翠絲是個出色的甜姐兒，她做什麼事都很精明——除了愛上班狄克這件事例外啦。」

說完，他就示意大夥繼續往前走，留班狄克在那裡思索所聽到的話。

班狄克偷聽得很起勁，當他聽到碧翠絲愛上他時，他喃喃自語道：「這有可能嗎？風會從那角落裡吹來嗎？」

P.110 待他們一行人離開後，班狄克開始推論說：「這不像是惡作劇啊，他們一派正經，話又是從希柔那裡聽來的，而且還一副很同情那位姑娘的樣子。她愛上了我！那我好歹要回應她，我沒想過要結婚，我說要打一輩子光棍，那是因為我不認為我這輩子會有結婚的一天。他們說那位姑娘德貌皆備，這也的確是啦。他們又說她凡事精明，只差愛上了我。喏，愛上我又不代表她蠢。哎呀，碧翠絲走來了，這位姑娘今天看來還真漂亮！我從她臉上瞧出幾分對我的愛意了。」

碧翠絲走近他，用慣有的尖酸語氣說：「要我叫你進屋吃飯，我是非常不情願的。」

班狄克沒想過自己會像現在這樣客氣地對她說話。他說：「美麗的碧翠絲，謝謝妳，辛苦了。」

碧翠絲又說了兩三句魯莽的話後離開。在她失禮的話語背後，班狄克認為他看到了她隱藏的柔情。於是他大聲說道：「我要是不心疼她，那我就是個大爛人。我要是不愛她，那我就是猶太人。我要弄張她的畫像來。」

P.112 這位先生就這樣掉進他們所設下的圈套，現在輪到希柔來設計碧翠絲了。為此，她差來她的兩個侍女烏蘇拉和瑪格莉特。她對瑪格莉特說：「好瑪格莉特，妳趕去客廳找我表姊碧翠絲，她現在正和親王及克勞迪說話。妳小聲地跟她說，我和烏蘇拉在果園裡散步，正在聊她的事。妳叫她偷偷躲在那個舒適的涼亭裡。太陽把那裡的金銀花曬熟，涼亭卻不准太陽進來，像個被寵壞的小孩。」

這個希柔要瑪格莉特誘使碧翠絲躲進去的涼亭，就是班狄克剛才在裡面偷聽到談話的涼亭。

「我保證一定馬上就讓她去。」瑪格莉特說。

P.114 希柔接著和烏蘇拉走進果園裡。她對烏蘇拉說：「烏蘇拉，現在一等碧翠絲來，我們就在這條小路上來回走，然後只聊班狄克的事。我會跟妳說班狄克對碧翠絲是如何地著迷，當我一提到他的名字時，妳就負責把他捧得好像他是天底下最棒的男人。我們現在就開始吧，妳看碧翠絲像隻貼地的田鼨，跑來偷聽我們的談話了。」

說罷兩人便開始。希柔好像回答烏蘇拉的什麼話似的，說道：「不，真的，烏蘇拉，她太瞧不起人了，她就像岩石上桀驁不馴的野鳥。」

烏蘇拉說：「妳確定班狄克真的迷上碧翠絲？」

希柔回答：「親王和我的未婚夫克勞迪都是這麼說的，他們要我轉告碧翠絲，但是我勸他們說，如果他們愛護班狄克，就不要讓碧翠絲知道這件事。」

P.115 「那當然。要是讓她知道了，那就不妙，她會冷嘲熱諷的。」烏蘇拉回答。

希柔說：「噯，說真的，不管是如何聰明、高貴、年輕或是俊俏的男人，她都會把他說得一文不值。」

「是啊，是啊，這麼挑剔實在不好。」烏蘇拉說。

P.116 「是很不好，但誰敢說她呢？要是我跟她說，我會被她譏笑得半死。」希柔回答。

「哦，妳誤會妳表姊了！她不會這麼沒有眼光，去拒絕一位像班狄克先生那樣難能可貴的紳士。」烏蘇拉說。

「他聲名是很好。說真的，除了我親愛的克勞迪之外，他是義大利最棒的男人了。」希柔說。

接著，希柔暗示侍女換話題。烏蘇拉說：「小姐，那您什麼時候要出嫁呢？」

希柔回答她明天就要嫁給克勞迪。她要烏蘇拉跟她一起去挑幾件新衣服，想叫她商量明天該穿什麼才好。

碧翠絲始終屏氣凝神地聽她們說話。待她們一走，她就叫說：「我耳朵怎麼這麼燙？這會是真的嗎？永別了，輕蔑與嘲諷！再會了，少女的高傲！班狄克，愛下去吧！我會回敬你的，用你柔情的雙手，馴服我一顆狂野的心吧。」

P.117 透過個性開朗的親王的趣味妙計，他們兩個人中了計，互相愛慕起對方。看到老冤家變成新交摯友，能目睹兩人互相中意後再見面的情形，一定很有趣，但我們現在先說希柔的不幸遭遇吧。明天本來應該是她的大喜日子，結果卻為希柔和父親李歐拿多帶來了悲哀。

親王有個同父異母的弟弟，和他一道從沙場回到梅西納。這個弟弟（名叫做唐降）個性陰鬱，貪心無厭，心裡頭總是在打著盤算。

P.118 他痛恨他的親王兄長。因為克勞迪與親王的交情很好，所以連帶地他也討厭克勞迪。他決定要阻撓克勞迪和希柔的婚事，讓克勞迪和親王痛苦，讓自己一逞幸災樂禍的痛快。他知道親王和克勞迪一樣，心思都放在婚事上。為了達到他缺德的目的，他雇用一個叫包拉喬的人。這人的心眼和他一樣壞，為了煽動這人，他用重金收買。

唐降知道包拉喬在追求希柔的侍女瑪格莉特，就要他讓瑪格莉特答應當天晚上在希柔睡著後，穿上希柔的衣服，然後在希柔閨房的窗口邊和他聊天，讓克勞迪誤以為她就是希柔，以完成這個缺德的陰謀。

之後，唐降去找親王和克勞迪，說希柔是個不知檢點的女人，三更半夜還在房間的窗口和男人聊天。

P.119 現在是婚禮前夕，他自告奮勇說今晚可以帶他們去看，讓他們親耳聽到希柔在窗邊和男人聊天。他們便跟著一道去，克勞迪說：「我今晚要是看到什麼讓我不該娶她的事，那麼明天，我就要在和她成婚的教堂裡當眾羞辱她。」

親王也說：「既然我幫助你追到她，那我也會跟你一起去羞辱她。」

當晚，唐降帶他們到希柔臥房的附近。他們看到包拉喬站在窗戶下面，瑪格莉特則從希柔的窗口往外看，他們還聽到她跟包拉喬說話。瑪格莉特穿的那套衣服，親王和克勞迪也都看過希柔穿過，因此兩人就認定那個人就是希柔小姐。

P.120 克勞迪（自以為）看到這件事後，非常憤怒。他對清白的希柔的感情，瞬間變成了恨。他決定如自己所說的，明天要在教堂裡揭發她。親王表示贊成，對於這個放蕩的姑娘，他認為不管什麼懲罰都不會過分，因為她在嫁給高貴的克勞迪的前一天晚上，還在窗邊和男人聊天。

隔天，大家都來到了婚禮上。克勞迪和希柔站在牧師面前（大家叫牧師為修道士），正當牧師要開始主持婚禮時，克勞迪用最激動的話語，宣布無辜希柔的罪狀。聽到他說這些莫名其妙的話，希柔很震驚。她溫和地說：「我的未婚夫還好嗎？他怎麼這樣胡言亂語？」

李歐拿多很吃驚，他對親王說：「殿下，您怎麼不說話？」

「我該說什麼？我才感到羞愧呢，竟撮合好友和一個不自重的女人結婚。李歐拿多，我以人格擔保，我、我弟弟和傷心的克勞迪，都看到而且聽到了她昨天半夜在房間窗口和男人聊天。」親王說。

P.122 班狄克聽了很詫異，他說：「這看起來不像是在舉行婚禮嘛！」

「的確，哦，天啊！」傷心的希柔回答道。說完，這個不幸的姑娘昏了過去，像是斷了氣一般。

親王和克勞迪不管希柔有沒有甦醒過來，也不理會他們帶給李歐拿多的痛苦，就逕自離開教堂。憤怒讓他們的心腸硬如鐵石。

班狄克留下來，幫助碧翠絲讓希柔醒過來。他說：「小姐還好吧？」

P.123 「我想是死了。」碧翠絲傷心地回答。她愛表妹，也清楚表妹的德性，壓根就不相信那些毀謗的話。

但那可憐的老父親就不是這樣了，他相信孩子做了丟臉的事。希柔像死屍一樣地躺在他面前，他希望她永遠都不要再睜開眼睛。聽著他的這般哀嘆，令人鼻酸。

老修道士是個明眼人，洞悉人性。當這位姑娘聽到自己被指控時，他細心留意她的神情。他先是看到她臉上漲滿羞愧的紅暈，接著天使般的白淨軀走了羞紅，他在她的眼裡看到某種火光，顯示親王指責她不貞的話子虛烏有。他對這個傷心的父親說：「躺在這裡的這位無辜的可愛姑娘，如果沒有受到天大的冤枉，那你就叫我笨蛋！不用再相信我的學問和見識，或是年歲、身分和職務！」

P.124 這時希柔從昏迷狀態中甦醒過來。修道士對她說：「姑娘，他們指控妳和哪個男人聊天？」

希柔回答：「他們那些指控我的人才知道，我不知道。」說完她轉向李歐拿多說：「哦，父親，如果您能證明有哪個男人曾在不合宜的時候和我說話，或是我昨晚和什麼人說過話，那您就別再認我，只管恨我，把我折磨到死吧。」

修道士說：「親王和克勞迪一定是有某種奇怪的誤會。」他建議李歐拿多宣告希柔已經去世，他們兩人離開希柔時，希柔昏死了過去，所以他們會信以為真。他勸李歐拿多穿上喪服，為她立碑，舉行完整的葬禮儀式。

「這會有什麼結果？」李歐拿多問：「這有什麼用呢？」

P.125 修道士回答：「宣告她的死訊，毀謗會轉為憐憫。這樣有好處，但我要的好處還不只這個。克勞迪要是得知自己的話逼死了她，那他腦海裡會溫柔地浮現出她的倩影。要是他真心愛過，他就會為她服喪。就算他真的認為自己的指控有憑有據，他還是會後悔自己那樣地指控她。」

這時班狄克說道：「李歐拿多，就聽修道士的忠告吧。雖然你也知道我很喜歡親王和克勞迪，但我以人格擔保，我不會跟他們洩漏這個秘密。」

經過勸說，李歐拿多答應了。他悲傷地說：「我太難過了，就連最小的細線都能把我牽走。」

P.127 好心的修道士帶李歐拿多和希柔離開，好好安慰他們，留下碧翠絲和狄克兩人。朋友們設計他們兩個人，想看他們現在見面的有趣樣子，結果卻變了調。大家現在一片愁雲慘霧，根本沒有尋歡作樂的心情。

班狄克首先開口說：「碧翠絲小姐，妳一直在哭嗎？」

「嗯，而且我還會再哭上一陣子。」碧翠絲說。

「是。我相信妳的好表妹被人冤枉了。」班狄克說。

「啊！能替她伸冤的人，才是我的朋友！」碧翠絲說。

「有什麼方法可以成為這種朋友？在這個世界上，妳是我最愛的人，我這樣說會奇怪嗎？」班狄克說。

碧翠絲說：「我也可以說我最愛的人是你，這不是謊話，但你不要相信我。我什麼都不承認，也不否認，我只為我表妹感到難過。」

P.128 「我用我這把劍發誓。妳愛我，我也正式宣告我愛妳！來，吩咐我為妳做些什麼事吧。」班狄克說。

「殺了克勞迪。」碧翠絲說。

「啊，那不可能啊！」班狄克回答。他愛克勞迪這個朋友，他相信他是被利用的。

「克勞迪這樣毀謗、蔑視、羞辱我的表妹，根本就是個流氓！我要是個男人就好了！」碧翠絲說。

「妳聽我說，碧翠絲！」班狄克說。

但碧翠絲根本不聽他為克勞迪所做的辯解。她仍催促班狄克為表妹申冤報仇，她說：「什麼和男人在窗邊聊天，說得好像真的一樣！親愛的希柔，她被冤枉誣告，她被毀了！哦，這個克勞迪，我要是男人就好了！要不然，有人願意為我當個男子漢也行！但是勇氣逐漸化成禮貌和恭維。我無法祈禱自己變成男人，我只能作女人家，然後傷心地死去。」

P.129 「等等，好碧翠絲。我舉手發誓我愛妳。」班狄克說。

「要是愛我，就用手做些別的事，不要用來發誓。」碧翠絲說。

「妳真的認為是克勞迪冤枉了希柔嗎？」班狄克問。

「是！這就像我有思想或靈魂一樣千真萬確。」碧翠絲回答。

「好，我決定去對他下戰書。離開妳之前，我要先親吻妳的手。我舉手發誓，一定要克勞迪給我一個的交代！請等我的消息，並且惦念著我。去安慰妳的表妹吧。」班狄克說。

碧翠絲懇求班狄克，用憤慨的話激起他的俠義之心，使他不惜為希柔去和好友克勞迪決鬥。就在這時，李歐拿多也要親王和克勞迪拿劍和他決鬥，因為他們傷害了他的孩子，讓她傷心而亡。兩人看著這個悲傷的老人，說道：「別這樣，我們不要決鬥，老好人。」

P.131 這時班狄克出現。克勞迪傷害了希柔，班狄克要他拿劍決鬥。克勞迪和親王對著彼此說道：「這是碧翠絲唆使的。」

就在這時，傳來了有力的證據，天理還給了希柔清白，要不然克勞迪會接受班狄克的挑戰，進行一場命運未卜的決鬥。

就在親王和克勞迪談著班狄克的挑戰時，一位地方法官將包拉喬當作犯人押到了親王面前。原來，包拉喬和友人聊起唐降雇用他去幹的勾當時，被旁人給聽到了。

P.132 克勞迪聽著包拉喬對親王的全盤招供。包拉喬說和他在窗邊聊天的人其實是瑪格莉特，她穿著小姐的衣服，讓他們誤以為是希柔小姐。克勞迪和親王於是不再懷疑希柔的清白，就算仍有疑心，也因唐降的潛逃而釋疑了。事跡敗露後，唐降為了躲開震怒的兄長，就逃離出梅西納。

P.133 克勞迪知道自己冤枉了希柔，他非常悲痛，自責自己無情的話逼死了她。心愛希柔的倩影，頓時浮現在他的腦海裡，那是他初愛上她時的樣子。親王問他，聽到事實時，他的心是否就像被燙過一樣。他回答，聽包拉喬說那些話時，他感覺自己好像在吞下毒藥。

悔恨不已的克勞迪懇求老李歐拿多原諒他帶給他孩子的傷害。他誤信對未婚妻的誣告，他允諾說，為了心愛的希柔，不管李歐拿多如何懲罰他，他都甘之如飴。

李歐拿多給他的懲罰是：隔天早上就娶希柔的一位堂親為妻。他說對方現在是他的繼承人，長相酷似希柔。因為是自己親口允諾的，克勞迪表示願意和這位不相識的姑娘成親，就算對方是個黑人也沒關係。

P.134 但他內心萬分哀傷，他在李歐拿多為希柔所立的墓碑前，懊悔悲痛，哭了一整夜。

到了早上，親王陪著克勞迪前往教堂。好心的修道士、李歐拿多和他的姪女都已經來到現場，準備慶祝第二場婚禮。李歐拿多把許配給克勞迪的新娘介紹給他，新娘子戴著面具，克勞迪看不到她的臉孔。

克勞迪對這位戴面具的姑娘說：「神聖的修道士在前，請妳把手交給我。妳若是願意嫁給我，我就是妳的丈夫。」

「我在世的時候，曾做過你妻子。」這位不知名的姑娘說。她揭開面具，原來她並非什麼姪女（如她所偽裝），而是李歐拿多如假包換的女兒希柔小姐。

克勞迪驚喜不已，他一度以為她死了。他興奮萬分，不敢相信自己的眼睛。親王看到這一幕也同樣吃驚，他大喊道：「這不是希柔嗎？不是那個已經死去的希柔嗎？」

P.136 李歐拿多回答：「殿下，她在被誣陷的時候，的確是死了。」

修道士答應說，婚禮結束之後，他會跟他們解釋這件奇蹟。當他正要開始主持婚禮時，班狄克打斷他，說他也要同時和碧翠絲成婚。

對這個婚事，碧翠絲有些異議。班狄克質問她不是愛他嗎？他聽到希柔這樣說的。在一番有趣的解釋過後，他們這才知道自己被設計，相信了對方的情意。他們本來無意，一場哄弄人的玩笑，竟讓他們弄假成真。

妙計誘騙他們互萌愛意，他們已經深深愛上對方，現在什麼也不能動搖他們的感情。既然班狄克求了婚，如今不管人們如何勸阻，也都沒有用。他開心地繼續這場玩笑。他對碧翠絲發誓說：他是因為可憐她才娶她，因為聽說她害相思病快死了。碧翠絲回嘴說：她答應嫁給他，是因為看在別人大力勸說的份上，想救他的小命，因為聽說他日形憔悴。

P.138 這兩個不拘小節的智多星就這樣和解。在克勞迪和希柔完婚後，他們也成親了。最後，把故事做個結尾吧。策動陰謀的唐降逃亡後被捕，押回了梅西納。對這個陰鬱而不安分的人來說，計謀失敗後，看到梅西納宮廷內喜氣洋洋地舉行盛宴，就是一種最嚴厲的懲罰了。